He tightened his arms around her as she began to weep. "Scarecrows...they were everywhere...chasing me. I was...in my car and then I was rolling upside down and downside up and...the scarecrows kept coming." Her words came with tearful gasps as she buried her face against his bare shoulder.

"Shh, you're okay now," he murmured against her ear. "You're safe here. It was just a bad dream."

She wrapped her arms more tightly around his neck. Despite her tears, he was acutely aware of her warm body intimately close against his. He could smell the scent of her that always stirred him.

Still, his desire was to comfort her and nothing more. He continued to hold her until her weeping finally stopped.

"I'm so sorry." She covered her face with her hands. "I'm so embarrassed."

"Why on earth would you be embarrassed?" He gently pulled at her hands to uncover her face. "Mary, you had a nightmare. There's nothing to be embarrassed about."

"Thank you, Lucas, for waking me up," she finally said and leaned towa~~d~~ ~~h~~~~e~~~~r~~ as if in invitation.

Dear Reader,

Welcome to Millsville, a small town in Kansas where the townspeople work together in a community with values like hard work and strong ethics.

This little town is much like the one where I grew up. It was built with farmers and shopkeepers. It's a place where time seems to move more slowly and friends and family are cherished.

However, a killer is at work and suddenly the young women of Millsville aren't safe anymore.

I hope you love this town as much as I do. It has secrets and danger, passion and, of course, love... always love!

Enjoy reading!

Carla Cassidy

KILLER IN THE HEARTLAND

Carla Cassidy

HARLEQUIN®
ROMANTIC SUSPENSE™

Recycling programs
for this product may
not exist in your area.

ISBN-13: 978-1-335-73811-0

Killer in the Heartland

Copyright © 2022 by Carla Bracale

For questions and comments about the quality of this book, please contact us at CustomerService@Harlequin.com.

Harlequin Enterprises ULC
22 Adelaide St. West, 41st Floor
Toronto, Ontario M5H 4E3, Canada
www.Harlequin.com

Printed in U.S.A.

Carla Cassidy is an award-winning, *New York Times* bestselling author who has written over 170 books, including 150 for Harlequin. She has won the Centennial Award from Romance Writers of America. Most recently she won the 2019 Write Touch Readers Award for her Harlequin Intrigue title *Desperate Strangers*. Carla believes the only thing better than curling up with a good book is sitting down at the computer with a good story to write.

Books by Carla Cassidy

Harlequin Romantic Suspense

The Scarecrow Murders

Killer in the Heartland

Colton 911: Chicago

Colton 911: Guardian in the Storm

Cowboys of Holiday Ranch

Cowboy at Arms
Operation Cowboy Daddy
Killer Cowboy
Sheltered by the Cowboy
Guardian Cowboy
Cowboy Defender
Cowboy's Vow to Protect
The Cowboy's Targeted Bride
The Last Cowboy Standing

Colton 911

Colton 911: Target in Jeopardy

Visit the Author Profile page at Harlequin.com for more titles.

Chapter 1

"Oh my gosh, I can't believe how many of those elevator thingies I saw when I was driving here. This whole town looks like something out of an old creepy movie." Heidi Barnell looked at Lucas Maddox with wide-eyed wonder.

"They're called grain elevators," Lucas replied dryly. He'd only known Heidi for about two minutes, but he already knew she wasn't right for the job.

As she'd breezed by him to come into his home, he'd smelled the distinct odor of marijuana clinging to her. He wasn't a judgmental kind of guy; he didn't care what choices people made for themselves. But he thought the young woman was high, and that instantly disqualified her from doing the job she was interviewing for.

"Heidi, did you bring a résumé with you?" Lucas asked.

"Yeah, I did." She flashed him a bright smile, swung one of her long pink-tinged braids over her shoulder and then dug into her oversize purse. She pulled out a wrinkled sheet of paper and tried to straighten it before handing it to him. "It's pretty brief," she admitted. "I haven't had a job in the last couple of years."

He had a feeling this was why she had insisted she didn't mind driving an hour and a half from Kansas City, Missouri, to his home in Millsville, Kansas, to interview in person. Maybe she was hoping her bright smile would automatically move her right into the position.

"This is a totally awesome house," she said as he pretended to read her very short résumé. "I wouldn't mind living here, even though the town is kind of old and small."

He glanced up from the piece of paper and smiled. "Thanks. We love it here."

"The corn is kind of creepy, but your house is awesome. Remember that old movie about the kids in the corn? It scared me for weeks after I saw it."

"The corn is just one of the things we grow around here. I've never found it particularly creepy," he replied, then smiled and stood. "I really appreciate you driving all the way out here. I'll keep your résumé here, although I'm still in the process of interviewing people."

She rose from the chair and followed him to his front door. "I didn't mind the drive. I love to roll my windows down and rock my music and just drive. It was nice to meet you, Mr. Maddock."

"It's Maddox," he corrected.

"Excuse me?" She smiled and eyed him blankly.

"Never mind. It was nice to meet you, too. Drive careful on the way home," he said.

He stood on the wraparound front porch and watched as she got into her car. He remained there until she drove down the long lane. As she disappeared from sight, another familiar vehicle headed toward his house.

He smiled and stepped down from the porch as his mother-in-law parked and got out of her car. He greeted her, and the two hugged.

"Who was that who just left?" she asked as they headed for the front door.

"A woman interviewing for the job." After entering the house, he led her into the kitchen. At least once a week or so, around four or five o'clock in the afternoon, Nicole stopped by for a cup of coffee and a chat.

"Is she a good prospect?" Nicole asked as she sank into one of the chairs at the table.

"Unfortunately, no." He set the coffee to brew and then sat down across from her. Nicole Dennis was an attractive older woman. Her dark hair and blue eyes were a constant reminder of her daughter, who had been the first and only love of Lucas's life.

She had been married to Raymond Dennis for years, and they had shared a small farmhouse with plenty of land around it. After Raymond had died ten years ago from a sudden heart attack, Nicole sold off most of the land but remained living on about five acres around her home.

Nicole had always been a slender, shapely woman, but in the past couple of years, she had gained a lot of weight. Still, she was quite attractive.

"How many does that make now?" she asked.

"Seven." He frowned. "You'd think out of seven women, I could find one who is appropriate for what I need."

Nicole shook her head ruefully. "I just wish I could still help out."

A month ago, Nicole had been diagnosed with a heart condition and, under her doctor's strict advice, could no longer help Lucas out. "I don't want your help. I want you to spend your time resting when you need to and following the doctor's orders. I'll just keep on interviewing until I find the perfect woman. She's got to be out there somewhere."

He got up and poured them each a cup of coffee and then returned to his seat across from her. "I've got the ad running locally starting tomorrow, and it runs for another week in the *Kansas City Star*."

"Maybe you should think about putting it in the

Topeka newspaper, too. That isn't so far from here," Nicole suggested.

"Maybe."

Nicole leaned across the table and patted the back of his hand. "I'm so proud of the way you've handled things, Lucas. More importantly, Diana would have been so wonderfully proud of you."

As always, Diana's name alone evoked the grief that had been with him for the past three years. Diana had been his everything…his best friend, his lover and his wife. Breast cancer had stolen her from his life, and not a day went by that he didn't miss her.

"Thanks, Nicole."

The patter of little feet and giggles broke the relative quiet of the kitchen. Three-year-old Annabelle flew into the kitchen, her black hair a curly mess and her blue eyes sparkling brightly.

"Granny!" she squealed, running toward Nicole. She clambered onto the older woman's lap and hugged her around her neck.

"Did you have a good nap, bug?" Lucas asked her.

Annabelle nodded and then smiled up at Nicole. "Did you bring me a present, Granny?"

"I'm sorry, sweetheart. I don't have a present for you today. Granny just didn't have time to go shopping for you this morning."

Annabelle's lower lip jutted out in a pout.

"Granny can't bring you a present every time she comes to visit," Lucas said, hoping to stave off one of his daughter's infamous tantrums.

"I think I might have a cherry piece of candy in my purse," Nicole said. She picked up her purse, withdrew a wrapped piece of candy and handed it to Annabelle.

"What do you say to Granny?" Lucas asked.

"Thank you, Granny." Annabelle slid off Nicole's lap. "Now I'm going to get my baby doll and play." She raced out of the kitchen, seeming to take much of the energy in the room with her.

"You spoil her," Lucas said.

Nicole smiled. "We both spoil her. When I look at her, I see Diana and I can't tell her no."

Lucas smiled. "I have the same problem. But I've got to start laying down some rules for her. Otherwise, she'll have problems when she gets into school."

"Ah, that's still two years away," Nicole replied. "You have plenty of time to whip her into shape. Besides, she's just like Diana was at that age, and she turned out all right."

Lucas smiled again. "She turned out absolutely perfect."

The two visited for another half an hour. After Nicole left, it was time for the usual routine of supper, a bath for Annabelle and then bedtime.

Hours later, he stood in the doorway of Annabelle's bedroom. She slept on her back, arms flung wide to each side as if ready to embrace all the wonderful adventures life had to offer her. As usual, she'd kicked off her covers, exposing her pink princess pajamas.

This little girl was his very heart and soul. He would positively die for her. His wife *had* died for her. Unbeknownst to him, Diana had been diagnosed with an aggressive form of breast cancer the same month she found out she was pregnant.

The doctor had suggested she abort the baby and treat the cancer, but Diana had chosen to carry Annabelle and put off treatment. Once Lucas had learned about her disease, he'd begged her to begin treatment, but Diana had been adamant in her decision to carry the baby and get treatment after the birth.

Unfortunately, by that time the cancer had spread aggressively. Three months after Annabelle's birth, Diana succumbed to the disease that had spread throughout her body, and she had passed away in his arms.

He wouldn't have gotten through the last three years without his baby girl and his mother-in-law. His own mother had passed away when he was sixteen. She'd suffered a brain aneurysm while cooking dinner one night and died almost immediately.

When Lucas turned eighteen, his father had given him the family home and the surrounding fields to work; then he'd taken off for California. The last time Lucas had spoken to his father, he was living on a houseboat and loving his life.

For the past three years, Nicole had watched Annabelle while Lucas worked the fields. But since Nicole's diagnosis a month ago, Lucas had been unable to get outside to work. Instead, he'd had to depend solely on the four men who worked part-time for him.

He released a deep sigh and left Annabelle's doorway. He walked down the hall to the large family room and moved to a back window with a view of his cornfields.

He smiled as he thought of Heidi's assessment of Millsville, Kansas. The "elevator thingies" she'd referred to were four large grain elevators Lucas and his neighbors shared. The corn was hardly creepy—it was a living. Right now, the corn was knee-high and right where it should be in early July.

Millsville wasn't creepy, either. It was a small town filled with farmers who depended on each other, men and women who worked hard in their fields and still enjoyed a good ice-cream social or dinner at the café.

There was also the Farmer's Club, the local bar where the people in town could hang out, have a few beers and blow off some steam. Hardly creepy.

He turned away from the window with a frown as the problem at hand rose up in his brain once again. Maybe he was being too picky. Maybe he was just expecting too much.

All he wanted was a live-in nanny who would cook and clean and take care of Annabelle. Not only would she have free room and board, but he also intended to pay her a generous salary. But he needed a respectable woman who loved children and would respect the rules of his home.

He didn't expect her to love Annabelle as much as he did. Nobody could do that. But surely there was one nice person—one special woman—who could add to their lives and allow him to work without worrying about his child's well-being.

All he could do was continue his search and hope and pray he found that woman soon.

Mary Curtis stared at the notice her landlady, Agnes Woodward, had slipped beneath her door that morning. She'd known it was coming. She'd known it ever since Agnes had put the three-bedroom house up for sale. Now the house had sold, and the new owners didn't want any tenants, which meant Mary had twenty days to vacate the premises.

She pushed the notice aside and sighed deeply. She had no idea where she might go. She'd lived here for the past ten years. When she'd moved in, she was a frightened eighteen-year-old who had just been told by her parents that it was time for her to move out of their home.

She now finally opened her bedroom door and padded down the hallway toward Agnes's kitchen. The older woman was seated at the round oak table with a cup of coffee in front of her. Agnes had been a loving mother figure for Mary these last ten years.

"Make yourself a cup of coffee and sit," Agnes said with a sad smile.

Mary poured herself a cup of the dark brew and then joined Agnes at the table. "It's okay, Agnes. I'll be just fine."

"I hope so. I'm really going to miss you, Mary. You've been like the daughter I never had."

Mary reached out and covered Agnes's gnarled hand with hers. "And you've been like the mother I never had. But you're doing what's best for you, and that's exactly what you need to do."

Agnes was a widow who had rheumatoid arthritis that was getting progressively worse. She had decided it was time to move to Indiana to be close to her son, who had been asking his mother to move closer for the past two years.

"Have you thought about where you'll move?" Agnes asked.

"No, but since today is my day off, I intend to use it to check out some places."

"You might try Etta Lawrence. I know she used to rent out rooms in her place. I don't know if she still does, but it might be worth it to stop by and talk to her," Agnes said.

"I'll keep that in mind." Mary looked at the clock on the wall. It was just after nine. "Are you finished with that?" She gestured to the folded newspaper on the table.

"I am." Agnes pushed the paper toward Mary.

"I thought I might see if anyone in town is advertising for a roommate," Mary explained.

"That's a good idea," Agnes agreed. "Just promise me one thing, Mary."

"What's that?"

"Promise me that you will continue on with your schooling so you can achieve your dream of becoming a full-time teacher."

"That's an easy promise to make," Mary replied with a smile. "It might be taking me a lot longer than other people, but eventually I'll get there."

"That's what I want for you. I want all the dreams you have for yourself to come true," Agnes replied.

The two women visited for another half an hour, and then minutes later, Mary was sprawled in the center of her bed with the paper opened in front of her. As she thumbed to the section she wanted to read, she thought about her promise to Agnes.

Her idea had always been to become a teacher and work with young children, but when her parents had offered her no financial help for college, she'd wound up taking a job as a checker at the grocery store. Despite having to pay rent to Agnes, she'd managed to sock away enough money to take a couple of classes online. When the money ran out, she worked for another few months until she had the funds for a couple more classes.

Finally, two years ago, she'd earned enough college credit hours to be able to substitute teach. Since then, she'd been substituting whenever she could and continuing to work as many hours as possible at the grocery store.

Her goal was to save up enough money to be able to quit working altogether and just focus on finishing up her education. But life kept throwing her curveballs. Like this latest one. She doubted she would ever find a place as lovely and as cheap as where she was living now.

She mentally shook herself. She wasn't going to get anything done if she continued to lie in the middle of her bed, lost in her thoughts.

Looking through the newspaper ads to find a room to rent was definitely depressing. She could find only one listed, and there was no way she would be renting a room from lecherous eighty-year-old Fred Stanley.

All the women in town knew to steer clear of Fred, who was likely to pinch a butt or sidle up beside you to invade your personal space. He was constantly asking young women to perform sex acts on him. She'd definitely rather live on the street than rent a room in Fred's house.

There was also the Millsville Motel, a rather dreary five-unit place that rented not only by the night but also by the week or month. If worst came to worst, she supposed she could rent a unit there for a while until she found something more appealing.

She scanned the page and stopped on an ad under the Help Wanted section. Lucas Maddox was looking for a live-in nanny and housekeeper? Her heart beat a little faster, and she read the ad again. Could this be a temporary answer to her situation?

A vision of Lucas danced in her head. He was definitely a good-looking man. His dark hair was slightly shaggy, and his eyes were a beautiful blue. His features were strong and masculine. And then there was his perfect body: broad shoulders and slim hips, long legs and... Oh, he was definitely a hunk.

She didn't really know him at all. She did know he had a beautiful little daughter, who was obviously the apple of his eye. She'd rung him up several times at the grocery store, and he'd always been quite pleasant. Still, she'd always felt unaccountably shy and slightly tongue-tied around him.

However, he might just be her answer as to where she could live. She'd dreamed of working with children, and she would love being a nanny to Annabelle. The more she thought about it, the more excited she was.

Could she convince him that she was perfect for the job? Was the position even still open, or had he already found somebody? She wouldn't find out any of those things unless she got up off the bed and got moving.

An hour later, she stepped out of Agnes's front door. The early-July midmorning heat slapped her in the face. Summers in Millsville were definitely hot and humid.

She got in the car and immediately turned on the air-conditioning. She'd decided to wear a pair of black slacks and a sleeveless button-up white blouse. With her long brown hair pulled into a braid down her back and just a touch of makeup, she hoped she looked professional and capable of doing the job Lucas Maddox needed to be done.

The closer she got to his farm on the outskirts of town, the more nervous she became. Maybe she should have called first. Maybe she should have set up an official interview with him. But her instinct had been just to show up on his porch and hope for the best.

She didn't know if she was nervous because she was going to talk to Lucas, whom she found incredibly attractive, or because it suddenly seemed absolutely vital that she get the job.

She turned right onto the country road that would take her to Lucas's sprawling spread. She knew that most farmers in this area grew wheat and corn and hay and milo, although she knew nothing about the actual growing of such crops. She didn't even know what milo was, but if she needed to, she could learn about it all.

And that was only if she got the job. She had no real references. Would he really want to hire somebody who had no experience being a nanny to his precious daughter?

She tightened her hands on the steering wheel as she passed an expansive field of corn, and then his house came into view. Lucas's home was a sprawling ranch with a wraparound porch. There were two chairs on the porch and a little pink riding toy. It created a vision that exuded welcome and warmth and family. All the things she had never had in her life.

She pulled up and parked in the middle of the circle driveway, right in front of the main door. She drew in several deep breaths for courage, then grabbed her purse and got out of the car.

A moment later, she stood in front of the door, once again gathering her courage to knock. She finally rapped on the door three times.

Lucas answered. "Mary," he said in obvious surprise. "Come on in."

"Thank you," she replied. *At least he knows my name*, she thought as she followed him through the foyer and into the living room.

"Please, have a seat." He gestured toward the overstuffed brown sofa. He looked totally hot in worn jeans and a navy T-shirt that stretched taut across his shoulders.

She sank down on the sofa, and he sat in a brown recliner facing her, wearing a look of curiosity. "I… uh…know I should have probably called first, but I'm here to apply for the job if it's still available."

Once again, he looked at her in surprise. "Uh…I didn't bring a résumé, and I don't have any references. But it's always been my dream to work with young children. I have been substitute-teaching at the elementary school whenever I can. I know how to cook and clean—but more importantly, I believe I can care for your daughter in a loving way." She talked fast, the words tumbling out of her mouth with passion.

"I'm a respectable woman," she continued. "You can ask anyone in town. You know I work at the grocery store, but I've also been taking online classes so I can get my teaching degree. Anyway, here's my contact information." She got up to hand him a small piece of paper, then returned to the sofa once again.

"So, you've never worked as a nanny before?" he asked.

"No, I haven't, but working as a substitute teacher is a little bit like being a nanny for the day. I teach the students and I love them," she replied. "You can call the school and ask them about my work there."

"And you would be available to move in here full-time?"

"Absolutely." She thought about telling him her situation, that she was going to be homeless in a matter of weeks, but then thought better of it. She wouldn't want him to think that the only reason she was here was to get a place to live.

"My daughter can be quite a handful," he said.

She smiled. "Most children that age can be a handful."

He studied her for a long moment and then smiled. "Mary, I appreciate you coming out to talk to me," he said. "I still have a couple of interviews set up in the next couple of days, but I will definitely keep you in mind."

She popped back up from the sofa. "I appreciate

you taking the time to speak with me." He also rose and walked with her back to the front door. He was close enough to her that she could smell his scent— one of sunshine and a fresh cologne that was very pleasant.

"Thanks again, Mary, for coming by," he said.

"Thank you again for taking the time to talk to me," she replied.

Minutes later, she was back in her car and headed home. A wave of depression descended on her. She was sure she wasn't going to get the job. He hadn't told her anything specific about it, and he hadn't even asked her many questions. He would probably find somebody who had worked as a nanny before, somebody who actually had a résumé and references.

She would have loved to be a nanny for Lucas's little girl, a precious child whose mother had passed away. But it undoubtedly wouldn't happen.

In her twenty-eight years, Mary had rarely gotten what she wanted. Her parents had been cold and distant, and she often wondered why they'd even had a child. Her childhood had been pretty sad and lonely. Maybe that was what had made her want to work with children in the first place.

She now felt more than a little embarrassed about asking Lucas for the job. She should have known he'd only want the very best for his daughter—and nobody had ever told Mary she was the very best. In any case, she hoped things weren't weird the next time she checked him out at the grocery store.

Now it was time for her to figure out where she was going to move. She hoped she could find a place that wouldn't eat up all her money to the point where she'd have to put off getting back to school even longer.

She felt as if she'd been scrambling for the past ten years to carve out a real life for herself, a life that didn't include living from paycheck to paycheck. By now she'd hoped to be working in her dream job and living in her own cozy little home.

Her new goal was to get her life together by the time she was thirty. She'd get through things with or without Lucas's job. She'd do it the way she always had: through hard work, perseverance and dedication. That was who she was. She shrugged the depression away as she focused on the next step in her life's journey.

Chapter 2

"I think I might have found somebody," Lucas said to Nicole the next afternoon. She had stopped by unexpectedly to check in on the quest for a nanny.

Nicole raised one of her dark eyebrows. "Did you interview somebody else this morning?"

"No, this was a complete surprise to me. Mary Curtis stopped by yesterday and wanted to apply for the job."

A frown danced across Nicole's forehead. "Mary Curtis? You mean that plain little checker from the grocery store?"

"Is she plain? I've never really noticed," Lucas said in surprise. "Anyway, she let me know she'd be interested in the job, and I think I'm going to hire her."

"Really? What are her qualifications? Has she been a nanny before? Does she have any references?" Nicole asked, her eyebrow shooting upward once again.

"No and no, but I just have a good feeling about her. She's been taking online classes to continue her education toward becoming a teacher. She's been substitute-teaching at the elementary school. She loves children, and she's a local with a good reputation. I'd feel better about hiring her rather than some total stranger."

Nicole took a drink of her coffee and then set the cup down. "Lucas, all I want is the very best for my granddaughter, and I know that's what you want. I support whatever decision you make, because I know you'll make that decision with Annabelle's well-being in mind."

"Thanks, Nicole. I plan on calling Mary later to see if she can come back and meet Annabelle—she was napping when Mary stopped by yesterday. That meeting will make up my mind about whether Mary is right for the job or not."

"I know how anxious you are to get back into the fields. I just wish I could still help you," Nicole replied mournfully.

"It's time for you to relax and enjoy your life, without any responsibilities except taking care of yourself. I'll be fine. If Mary doesn't work out, I still have a few more interviews set up. I'll find the right person."

"I hope so," Nicole said.

It was just after lunch when Lucas sat down on the sofa while Annabelle played with baby dolls in the middle of the living room floor.

He'd thought about Mary all night long. When he'd sat down with her the day before, it was obvious that she was extremely nervous. But beneath the nerves, her passion to get the job had been palpable.

It was funny to him that Nicole had described her as plain. He'd only seen Mary with her long hair in a braid or a bun, but he imagined her brown locks were quite pretty when they were loose.

Her green eyes were vivid and bright. He found her attractive in a quiet, unassuming way. However, it didn't matter if she was a wildly sexy woman and he was physically attracted to her or not—the last thing he wanted was any kind of a romantic or personal relationship with another woman.

Diana had been his heart and soul. Her memory would forever burn bright in his heart, and that was enough for him. He'd had the perfect woman for him, and there was no way he wanted to replace her with anyone else.

"Daddy, look—baby is sleeping in her crib," Annabelle said.

Lucas looked in the little pink plastic crib, where she'd put her baby to sleep. "She looks very comfy," he said. "Daddy has to make a phone call. Can you be quiet while I talk on the phone?"

"'Kay," Annabelle replied. "But hurry 'cause I need to sing to my baby."

"I promise I won't be long," he agreed. He grabbed his phone and the paper with Mary's contact information. He had a good feeling about Mary, but he couldn't make a decision until he saw her interact with Annabelle.

She answered on the second ring. "Mary, it's Lucas Maddox."

"Oh, hi, Mr. Maddox," she replied.

"Please, call me Lucas. Mary, I was wondering if you'd be available to come back out here around three this afternoon to meet with me and Annabelle for a little while."

"Of course. I'll be there promptly at three. Thank you, Lucas."

She hung up before he could say anything else. Apparently, she was a woman of few words, and that wasn't all bad. The last thing he'd want in his home was an overly chatty woman who didn't know the value of silence.

It was almost three o'clock when Annabelle awakened from her nap. She had moved from playing baby doll to building towers with oversize, lightweight blocks when a knock fell on the door.

A burst of nerves shot off in Lucas's stomach, surprising him as he got up to answer the door. God, he really wanted this to work out. He was desperate to find a good nanny so he could get back out in the fields.

"Hi, Mary," he said in greeting. "Please, come on in." He opened the door wider to allow her entry. She nodded, and as she swept past him, he caught the scent of fresh flowers, the strongest note being that of pleasant lilacs.

Once again, she was wearing black slacks, but today she'd paired them with a sleeveless blouse that was the color of new green grass, making her green eyes appear even more vivid.

He didn't have to worry about making introductions between Mary and Annabelle. Mary walked into the great room and immediately clapped her hands together. "What a wonderful tower, Annabelle," she said. "Did you make it all by yourself?"

Annabelle nodded proudly. "You the lady from the grocery store," she said.

"That's right. My name is Mary, and I'm here to visit with you for a little while."

"Not to visit with my daddy?" Annabelle asked with a curious frown.

"Not right now." Mary sat down on the floor. "I just want to visit with you."

"Did you bring me a present?" Annabelle asked.

Mary shot a quick glance at Lucas and then looked back at Annabelle. "The present is that I'd like to play with you for a little while."

Annabelle frowned once again, and Lucas held his breath, waiting for one of his daughter's melt-downs. Annabelle suddenly smiled and clapped her hands together. "That's a nice present. Do you want to play baby dolls?"

"I'd love to play baby dolls," Mary replied.

For the next thirty minutes Lucas watched the two interact. He'd always believed Mary to be a quiet and reserved woman, but with Annabelle, she was lively and totally engaged. Mary had a musical laugh; more than once, she and Annabelle dissolved into giggles.

By the time thirty minutes had passed, Lucas had made up his mind. "Annabelle, can you go play in your room for a little while? Mary and I need to have a grown-up talk."

"Can't I play with Mary for a few more minutes?" Annabelle asked. "Just five more minutes, Daddy? Just five...'kay?" She gave him her best charming, cajoling smile.

"Okay, five more minutes," Lucas said.

He gave them five more minutes and then finally got Annabelle to take her baby dolls and go to her room. "Why don't you come on into the kitchen?" he suggested once Mary got up from the floor.

She followed him in, and he gestured toward a seat at the table. "Can I get you something to drink? Coffee or maybe a cold soda."

"No, thank you. I'm fine," she replied.

He sat across from her. Once again, he felt her nervous energy radiating toward him. "What do you think about Annabelle? Can you see yourself spending your days with her?"

Mary smiled. The gesture didn't just involve her

lips but lit up her eyes as well. "She is absolutely delightful. She's obviously bright and very verbal. And yes, I can see myself spending my time taking care of her."

"Let me tell you more about what the job entails. Not only would I expect you to take care of Annabelle while I'm in the fields each day, but I would also need you to cook an evening meal and clean the house. Once dinner is finished, you are off duty. You also have the weekends off." He explained to her more about what he expected and then told her the salary he was offering.

Throughout the conversation, he found it impossible to read her. She held eye contact with him but gave no sign as to whether she was now really interested in the job or not.

Maybe she hadn't really liked Annabelle. Maybe she thought the little girl would be too much of a handful, and she now wasn't interested in the job. There was no question that Annabelle was a bundle of energy.

"Needless to say," he continued, "you would have your own bedroom, and if you have anything that needs to be stored, I have a barn and a shed that could be used. So…uh…what do you think?"

"I'd love to come and work for you," she replied simply.

A wave of utter relief fluttered through Lucas. He felt good about this. "When would you be available to start?" he asked.

"As soon as you want me to," she answered.

"How about tomorrow? Is that too soon? It will be Saturday, and you would be off duty, but you could take the weekend to settle in and get familiar with everything."

"Okay," she said. "However, if I'm going to do that, then I better get home and start packing." She rose from the table and he did as well.

Annabelle ran in from her bedroom. "Are you going to play with me again?" she asked.

"Mary has to go home now," Lucas said. "But how would you feel about Mary coming to live with us and taking care of you?"

Annabelle frowned and looked up at Mary. "Will you play with me?"

Mary bent down so that she was on Annabelle's level. "Absolutely, I'll play with you. We'll have playtime, and we'll have work time. So what do you think? Would you like me to move in here with you and your father?"

"And you'll play baby dolls with me?"

Mary laughed, and once again, Lucas was aware of how musical and filled with joy her laughter was. "Yes, we'll have lots of time to play baby dolls."

"Then move in…move in…move in!" Annabelle chanted and danced around Mary.

Lucas and Mary laughed. They finally said their goodbyes and she left. Annabelle went back to her room to play, and Lucas returned to the kitchen.

He poured himself a cup of coffee and then sat

down at the table. For the first time in a long time, he felt like he'd gotten a lucky break.

Mary seemed perfect, even though he didn't know her well. Yes, she seemed absolutely perfect... But he knew well the capriciousness of fate, and he hoped he hadn't just made the biggest mistake of his life.

Mary packed the last suitcase into the back of her car and then returned to the house to tell Agnes goodbye.

"Is that the last of it, then?" Agnes asked when Mary came into the kitchen.

"I think so," Mary answered. "You can call me if you find anything I've left behind."

"At least I know you're going to be living in a beautiful home and working for a respectable man," Agnes said, getting up from the table to walk Mary outside.

"He does seem nice, and his daughter is a real cutie—and the salary he offered me on top of the free room and board is very generous."

"Oh, Mary, I'm so happy this is working out the way it is for you," Agnes replied. "Now I can move to Indiana and not worry about you."

"Now, Agnes, have I ever given you a reason to worry about me?" Mary asked teasingly.

"Only once...when you got that creepy cyber-stalker. Is he still bothering you?" A frown creased the older woman's forehead.

"No, he isn't bothering me anymore." It was a

little white lie meant to waylay Agnes's concerns. The last thing Mary wanted was for Agnes to worry about her at all as they both started their new journeys through life.

"And of course, we'll stay in touch by phone," Mary added as the two of them stepped out onto the front porch. Emotion rose up inside her as she faced Agnes.

The older woman had taken a chance on an eighteen-year-old girl who'd had nothing except enough money for the first month's rent. Without Agnes, Mary had no idea where she would be right now.

"I guess I'd better head out," Mary finally said before sadness could overtake her. Agnes pulled her in for a tight hug.

"You take care of yourself, girl." Agnes patted Mary's back. "Maybe you will wind up married to Lucas, and you'll live happily ever after."

She stepped back, and Mary laughed. "That's certainly not going to happen. Lucas is strictly my boss and will never be anything more to me. Now, speaking of Lucas, it's time for me to get out to his place. Thank you, Agnes, for believing in me even when I wasn't sure I believed in myself."

"You were not only the best tenant I ever had, but you know I love you, Mary." Agnes pulled a tissue out of the top of her blouse and dabbed at her eyes.

"I love you, too, Agnes, and I'll call you once I get settled in." Mary turned and headed for her car, refusing to look back for fear she'd start to cry.

She would miss Agnes, who had supported her and loved her through these last ten years when there had been no parental love for her. However, now it was time for Mary to think about her immediate future.

Thoughts of her future had kept sleep at bay the night before. She'd tossed and turned, teased by visions of moving in with Lucas Maddox. After all, she really knew very little about him.

She knew he'd lost his wife right after his daughter had been born, but she'd never heard about him dating anyone. In fact, she'd never heard any kind of gossip where he was concerned. She could only hope he was exactly what he seemed to be—a pleasant and respectable man.

It was a nice drive from the center of town to Lucas's place. The farmlands she passed were rich with the color of the various growing crops and looked beautiful against the backdrop of a clear blue sky.

She loved living in Millsville and had never wanted to live anyplace else. She enjoyed the small-town community atmosphere. From working in the grocery store, she knew practically everyone in town by name, and she'd heard a lot of rumors, most of which she dismissed with a grain of salt.

Her heart accelerated as she saw the cornfields that indicated Lucas's house was just ahead. She couldn't help but be nervous. She'd jumped into this job without any backup plan. If for some reason this didn't work out, she would not only be out of a job but also a place to live.

She checked the time on her dashboard: nine o'clock. There was another car parked in the driveway, and as she pulled up to park behind it, Lucas immediately stepped outside the door. It was as if he'd been standing by the door, just watching and waiting for her to arrive.

"Good morning," he said as she got out of the car.

She tried not to notice how fine he looked with the sun shining in his thick dark hair and a wide smile curving his sensual lips.

"Good morning to you, too." She offered him a shy smile. "I hope I'm not too early for all this."

"Not at all. I made the mistake of telling Annabelle at breakfast this morning that you were moving in today, and she's been bugging me since then, wanting to know when you were going to get here."

Mary smiled. "I'm eager to see her, too."

"Okay, then, let's get you unpacked."

Mary punched the button on her key ring to open the trunk of her car. Lucas looked inside and then turned back to her. "Do you have more things coming?"

"No…uh…this is it." How pathetic was it that a twenty-eight-year-old could fit everything she owned into two suitcases, a carry-on bag and a box?

"Okay, let's get this all inside, and you can get settled in," he said.

He picked up the two suitcases and she grabbed the

small carry-on bag. She'd have to come back out to get the box. The minute she stepped into the house, Annabelle came running into the great room, followed by Nicole Dennis, who Mary knew was Lucas's mother-in-law.

"Mary…Mary, come play with me," Annabelle said.

"Remember what I told you, Annabelle?" Nicole said.

Annabelle frowned and then brightened. "Ms. Mary—right, Granny? I'm 'posed to call her Ms. Mary."

"That's right." Nicole smiled at Annabelle and then at Mary. "It's nice to see you here, Mary."

"Thank you. It's nice to be here."

"Let me show you to your room," Lucas said.

He led the way down a long hall. Mary followed behind him, and Annabelle danced after her. At the end of the hall, he went into a bedroom that contained a queen-size bed covered with a peach-colored spread.

There was a chest of drawers with a television on top and a dresser with an artificial-flower arrangement in peaches and greens and white. The room even had a writing desk that would provide a perfect place for her to set up her computer.

"Oh, this is all quite lovely," she said as he set the suitcases down at the foot of the bed.

"Thanks. There's a walk-in closet and a full bathroom." He pointed to the two doorways. "The television gets the same channels as all the other televisions

in the house. Do you think you can be satisfied here?"
He gazed at her intently, as if afraid she might turn
up her nose at the accommodations.

"I will definitely be satisfied," she replied. "This
is very nice."

He seemed to expel a sigh of relief; then he turned
around and leaned down to Annabelle, who had followed them into the room. "This is Ms. Mary's room,
and when she's in here, we can't bother her. The only
way you can come in this room is if she invites you
in. Do you understand?"

Annabelle nodded. "But she'll still play with me?"

"Of course I will," Mary answered the little girl
with a smile. "We'll have lots of time to play."

"Can we play now?" Annabelle asked.

"Ms. Mary is going to unpack, and she doesn't
start working for us until Monday. That's two days
away," Lucas said to his daughter.

"I'm sure I can find time to play with you a little
later today," Mary said.

Annabelle clapped her hands together. "And we'll
play baby dolls, 'kay?"

Mary laughed. "Okay."

"And now we're going to leave Ms. Mary alone
so she can get unpacked," Lucas said. "I'll get the
box from your trunk and carry it in for you," he said
to Mary.

"Thank you. I appreciate that," Mary replied.

"And we'll have a chat later," Nicole said to Mary.

Minutes later, Mary was alone in the room. She

sank down on the edge of the bed and looked around the fairly spacious room where she would be living for an undetermined amount of time.

On the nightstands, there were two attractive twin lamps that she knew would create soft, glowing light. There were two windows in the room; she got up from the bed to check out her view.

The first window faced the cornfields, and the second looked out over the backyard. There was a nice fenced-in yard with a fancy pink-and-white play-house. She could also see the edge of what appeared to be a large back patio.

She let the gauzy white curtain fall back into place and then explored the bathroom. It, too, was nicely decorated in peach and white. The linen closet held plenty of towels in various sizes, and the peach-colored shower curtain looked crisp and new.

She finally turned to her suitcases and set about unpacking. There were plenty of hangers in the closet, so she hung what she could and then placed her other items in the dresser drawers.

The box held a variety of knickknacks and mementos she'd gathered through the years. There were also some supplies she'd specifically bought for this job the evening before, such as crayons and drawing paper, bright colorful stick-on stars and other items to use as rewards for a little girl.

There was nothing in her things from her parents. They had given her a cheap car and two suitcases for her eighteenth birthday when they'd told her it was time to move out.

Still, she had a beautiful purple vase that Agnes had given her on her twenty-fifth birthday, along with a funny-looking ceramic frog, also from Agnes. When Agnes had given her the frog, she'd told Mary that she hoped she wouldn't have to kiss too many frogs before finding her prince.

Unfortunately, Mary had kissed a couple of frogs, and she'd given up looking for a prince. Her last attempt had been with a man on an internet dating site, where a pleasant beginning turned into a nightmare. After that, she'd decided to focus on getting her life together before she ever thought about a romantic relationship again.

By noon, she was all unpacked. Even though she'd told Annabelle she would play with her, Mary wasn't sure if she should leave the room or not.

She'd been sitting on the edge of her bed for about a half an hour when a knock fell on her door. It was Lucas. "Lunch is ready, if you want to come eat with us," he said.

"I'd love to," she replied and followed him down the hallway.

"Ms. Mary!" Annabelle squealed. "Are we gonna play?"

"No, my little bug. We're going to eat some lunch now." Lucas picked Annabelle up and threw her over his shoulders.

"Daddy, I not a bug," Annabelle said amid giggles. Lucas carried her to the big, airy kitchen, and Mary wondered if this was where Nicole had fixed the meal before leaving.

"Did Mrs. Dennis leave?" she asked.

"Yes, she had to go," he replied.

He deposited Annabelle in her booster seat at the round oak table and then gestured toward a chair for Mary. She knew there was a formal dining room, as they'd passed it on her way in, but this table, which seated four, was much more intimate for family dining.

There was a tuna-noodle casserole in the center of the table, along with a bowl of peas and a red gelatin salad filled with fruit. "This looks really good. Did Mrs. Dennis make this before she left?"

Lucas sat down in the chair across from her and shook his head. "Actually, Celeste Winthrop dropped this off yesterday. Occasionally, a woman from town will drop by to visit, and they often bring food. I guess they're afraid that Annabelle might starve if left to my cooking. Please, help yourself."

Mary was pretty sure the women weren't worried about Annabelle's dining habits. She would imagine there was quite a casserole brigade of single women coming to see the very handsome widower.

It would be good if Lucas married again, especially if he could find a woman who not only loved him but also loved his daughter as well.

"You'll have to tell me what you enjoy eating so I'll know what to cook for you," she said.

"No peas, Daddy," Annabelle said as Lucas placed a spoonful of the little green vegetables on her plate.

"You know the rule, Annabelle," he replied.

"What's the rule?" Mary asked curiously.

"She has to eat three bites of vegetables at lunch and at dinner," Lucas replied.

"No peas," Annabelle said more forcefully. Her nose wrinkled, and her bottom lip jutted out.

"Come on, honey. Just three little bites." Lucas looked at his daughter, shot an embarrassed glance at Mary and then turned back to Annabelle.

She raised her little chin, picked up several peas with her fingers and then threw them to the floor. Mary couldn't help the small gasp of shock that escaped her.

"Oh, Annabelle." Lucas got up from his chair to pick up the peas from the floor. "Eat the tuna and noodles," he told his daughter as he retook his seat and placed the errant peas by the side of his plate.

Mary made a note to have a discussion with him about discipline. "Now, where were we?" he asked as his cheeks flushed with color.

"I was telling you that you need to tell me what kind of food you like to eat so I'll know what to cook for you," she repeated.

"I'm really not a picky eater. I pretty much like everything. I've arranged for Nicole to be here on Monday to kind of walk you through your first official day of work. But in the meantime, feel free to get into the kitchen and explore."

"I might do that. Now that I'm unpacked, I really don't have much to do with my time."

"I encourage you to explore the whole house and get familiar with your surroundings."

"I like red stuff," Annabelle said. "Ms. Mary, I like red stuff." To prove her point, Annabelle took a big bite of the gelatin salad.

"That's good to know. I like it, too." Mary smiled at the little girl. "But I also like peas." To prove her point, Mary took a bite of the peas.

Annabelle eyed the peas on her plate and then scooped three of them into her spoon and ate them. "I like peas, too, Ms. Mary."

"That was a quick change of heart," Lucas observed with obvious surprise.

Mary grinned at him. "I'm new and it looks like somebody wants to please me. Trust me—that will change with more familiarity."

The rest of lunch passed pleasantly as Lucas told her about the daily routines, both for him and for his daughter.

"I'll help you with the cleanup," Mary said when they'd finished eating.

"Nonsense. You aren't on duty yet," he replied.

"Really, I don't mind."

With Lucas's help, Annabelle got down from the table and ran to her room to play while Mary and Lucas cleared the table. "There's one thing we haven't discussed yet," she said once everything from lunch was put away.

"What's that?"

When his beautiful blue eyes held her gaze so intently, a faint fluttering went off in her heart. Lordy, but the man was good-looking. And what was even sexier was the fact that he appeared completely unaware of just how attractive he was.

"Mary?"

She started as a blush warmed her cheeks. Jeez, how long had she been standing and staring at him? "I'm sorry. I was…uh…just thinking. Anyway, we haven't talked about discipline."

He winced, the gesture doing nothing to detract from his handsomeness. "Ah, as you probably noticed at lunch, I'm not very good at it, but she definitely needs some. However, I don't believe in spanking."

"I don't believe in spanking, either," she assured him. "But are you good with time-outs and consequences for her actions? Such as, 'if you don't eat your peas, then you don't get dessert'?"

"I'm completely fine with all of that," he replied.

"You do realize that follow-through is the key. Initially, she will probably cry and wheedle and do everything in her power to get her way. Lucas, I don't want to overstep my boundaries, so if you see something you don't like in the way I'm doing things, then by all means, tell me. Just don't tell me in front of Annabelle." She flushed. "Sorry, I'm probably talking too much."

"No, not at all," he assured her with one of his beautiful smiles. "It sounds like we're both on the same page with the discipline issue. You just tell me what I need to do. Annabelle can be a charming, delightful child, but she can also be a little hellion when she doesn't get her way. Nicole and I both realize we've failed in this particular area."

"Still, you've succeeded tremendously in the love department. It's obvious that Annabelle feels very loved and secure, and that's what's really important," she replied.

"Thanks, Mary. Annabelle is my very heart. And now I'm going to go get her into bed for her nap."

As he left the kitchen and headed for Annabelle's room, Mary returned to her own. Once there, she set up her computer on the desk and connected to the Wi-Fi with the password he'd given her earlier.

Before checking her email, she just sat for a few moments and replayed the conversations she'd had with Lucas. Of course, she still didn't know him well, but at the moment, she had to admit she was entertaining a bit of a crush on her employer.

It was totally inappropriate, and she certainly knew it would never go anywhere, nor should it. Hopefully, spending more time with him would make the silly crush go away. With a sigh, she went to her email.

Her blood immediately chilled. Twenty messages. There were twenty messages from *him*—a man named Kenny Majors, who'd been cyberstalking her for months.

She had stopped responding to him as soon as he had gotten verbally abusive. She'd hoped he'd just move on, but that hadn't happened yet. These new messages were filled with nasty words and threats.

She deleted all the emails and then shut down her computer. She released a deep sigh and then got up and moved to the window that looked out on the corn. There was one man in her life who frightened her because she didn't know how dangerous he might be, and there was another man she liked but couldn't develop any further feelings for…because she *knew* it would be dangerous.

Chapter 3

"Lucas takes his coffee black, and when he takes the occasional day off, he loves pancakes and bacon for breakfast," Nicole said. The two women sat in the kitchen, each of them with a cup of coffee. It was just after seven on Monday morning. Lucas had left for work, and Annabelle was still asleep.

The older woman looked attractive in a royal blue blouse and black slacks. The color of the blouse really made her bright blue eyes pop.

Mary had a notebook open in front of her and was taking copious notes as Nicole told her what Lucas and Annabelle liked and disliked.

From breakfast food to lunch and dinner, Nicole then moved on. "Lucas doesn't like a lot of chatter.

Aside from spending time with Annabelle, he's really a solitary kind of man who enjoys a quiet house, especially in the evenings."

Mary was vaguely surprised by this. Lucas had been quite talkative to her all day the day before. "I'll definitely keep that in mind," she said.

"You know, he and my daughter were childhood sweethearts, and their love and devotion to each other never wavered through the years." Nicole's blue eyes got misty. "Theirs was a wonderful love story—so much so that I know he won't ever marry again. He still loves my daughter, and she'll always be in his heart…in his very soul."

Her words suddenly sounded like a warning to Mary. Nicole needn't worry. Mary wasn't entertaining the thought of having any kind of a personal relationship with Lucas. Besides, she knew the depth of Lucas's love for his deceased wife.

Diana's pictures hung on several walls around the house. She had been a beautiful woman with thick dark hair and bright blue eyes. Annabelle was the spitting image of her mother, and Mary was sure looking at the little girl probably brought Nicole and Lucas both enormous pleasure and exquisite pain.

Nicole went on to tell Mary how Lucas liked his clothes washed and hung, what softener to use on Annabelle's clothes and more about laundry than Mary really needed to know.

Nicole finally left at noon as Mary was making grilled-cheese sandwiches for Annabelle's lunch. If

Mary was being honest, it wasn't a minute too soon. While the older woman was very nice, it was obvious she was still deep in the grieving process over her daughter. Mary was sympathetic; the loss of a child at any age must be devastating.

After lunch, Annabelle and Mary went to the little girl's room to play. They played for about an hour, and then Mary announced it was Annabelle's nap time. "Can't we play for just a little bit longer?" Annabelle pleaded. "Just five more minutes, 'kay? Five more minutes."

"Five more minutes, and then you promise you'll get in bed and take a nap, okay?"

"'Kay," Annabelle agreed.

Mary was surprised that Annabelle went down for her nap without a fight. Five minutes later, the little girl was sound asleep, and Mary went into the kitchen to start on dinner preparations.

She was a bit nervous in that tonight would be her first meal for Lucas in her official role as housekeeper. Thankfully, Mary enjoyed cooking and considered herself to be pretty good at it. She had cooked many evenings for Agnes, who had encouraged her to try her hand at a variety of dishes.

"Just consider me your guinea pig," Agnes would say with a twinkle in her eyes. "Cook away and I'll try anything you make."

Tonight, Mary was making Swiss steak, mashed potatoes and green beans, with the leftover gelatin salad. Mary hoped the steak was nice and tender, and she hoped Lucas liked it.

Annabelle slept until just after three. Mary knew the minute she was awake, for she danced into the kitchen with giggles and smiles. "Come play with me, Ms. Mary?"

"It's not playtime right now. It's work time," Mary replied.

"Work time?" Annabelle looked at her curiously. "What work time?"

"I thought you might like to set the table so that when your daddy gets home, we can eat dinner."

"Set the table? I don't know that." Annabelle reached up and grabbed a piece of her hair and twirled it.

"Don't worry, Annabelle. I'll show you," Mary replied with a smile.

The first thing Mary did was pull out the crayons and a large piece of paper. At the top, she wrote "Annabelle's Chores." She divided a chart into the days of the week and then showed the package of stars to the child.

"You get a star when you help me and Daddy, or you could also get a star for extra-good behavior. When you get ten stars, then you get a little present from the store."

Annabelle clapped her hands together. "I like presents. I want to get ten stars."

"You can earn one by setting the table, okay?"

"'Kay," Annabelle replied eagerly.

They then began to set the table. With each item Annabelle placed on the table, she squealed with excitement, ecstatic over the idea of telling her daddy how much she had helped and about earning her very first star.

Mary had always believed you disciplined children by telling them what they were doing right and not by punishing them when they did wrong. If ultimately she did have to punish, the time-out chair and learning about consequences would be enough.

She also believed in having conversations with children, not yelling at them. Since she had never done this before in real life, she could only hope her theories worked well.

She sat Annabelle in the empty seat at the table with crayons and another piece of paper. "While I'm cooking, why don't you color a nice picture for your daddy?" she said. "I'm sure he would like that."

"'Kay," Annabelle agreed eagerly.

While they each worked at their "jobs," Annabelle kept up a running chatter. They talked about pets; she wanted a baby aardvark. She told Mary all the names of her baby dolls, and there were a lot of them. She asked about Mary's mommy and daddy, and then she told Mary that her mother was up in heaven. "Daddy said she's a angel that watches over us."

"I'm sure that's true," Mary agreed. Her heart broke for Annabelle and the mother she had lost so early in her life. Annabelle hadn't had the chance to know a mother's love in her life.

By the time Lucas walked through the back door, dinner was ready. "Daddy, I drewed you a picture," Annabelle announced.

"You drew me a picture?" Lucas walked over to the table to look at his daughter's artwork. "Honey, that's great," he said.

Annabelle jumped off her chair, grabbed Lucas's hand and pulled him to the refrigerator, where the chart of stars that Mary had made hung on the door with little ladybug magnets.

"And look, I got a star, and when I get ten, Ms. Mary will buy me a present," she said.

"Oh, a star." Lucas shot a quick glance at Mary and then looked back at his daughter. "Why did you get a star?"

"I setted the table," she announced proudly. "It was my work."

"You set the table?"

Annabelle nodded vigorously.

"All by yourself?" he asked.

"All by myself, and Ms. Mary helped me," she replied.

Lucas laughed. "That's wonderful, Annabelle. I'm so proud of you." He leaned down and gave her a kiss on the cheek.

"And dinner is ready whenever you are," Mary said.

"Just let me go take a quick shower, and then I'm ready," he replied.

"Annabelle, you need to put the crayons away, and

I'll help get you into your chair for dinner," Mary said. She tried to ignore the nerves that danced in her veins. Gosh, she hoped Lucas liked what she had cooked. She also hoped he supported the star system she'd implemented even though she hadn't spoken to him about it first.

By the time he walked back into the kitchen fifteen minutes later, Annabelle was buckled in her booster seat and Mary had the meal on the table.

"Mmm, something smells really delicious," he said and gestured toward the chair opposite him.

Something definitely smelled good. Lucas smelled of sunshine and minty soap and the faint scent of clean, fresh cologne.

"This looks great, Mary," he said and smiled at her.

"I hope it tastes as good as it looks," she replied.

They filled their plates, and after a bite of the steak, he complimented her. She relaxed a bit. Thank goodness he liked it.

"So, how was your day?" she asked.

"Oh, it was good," he replied, as if surprised she had asked. "And how did your day go?"

As they ate, Annabelle filled him in on their playtime, and Mary explained her star system to him.

"I like it," he said. "However, when she gets to ten stars, I'll give you money to buy the reward."

"No, please. I insist that I take care of this," Mary said in protest.

"Are you sure?"

"I'm positive," she replied firmly. "This is my program, and I'll take care of it."

"Okay, then, the lady will have her way," he replied with a grin.

"Thank you." A hot blush filled her cheeks. She hoped that with more time, she wouldn't be so struck by how handsome he was or how his smiles made a pool of warmth in the pit of her stomach.

For the rest of the meal, they continued to talk about innocuous things...the weather and his work. "Did you know your daughter wants a pet aardvark?" she asked when there was a lull in the conversation.

"Aardvark!" Annabelle exclaimed. "I want a baby aardvark!"

Lucas released a sigh. "Yes, I know. *Andy the Adventurous Aardvark.* It's a children's show on television."

"Ah, now it all makes sense," Mary replied with a laugh.

"I guess I should be happy that it isn't Elmer the Exciting Elephant," he said, making Mary laugh again.

When they'd finished eating, he started to clear the table, but she stopped him. "I'm on duty now. You go play with your daughter, or just take the time and relax." She took the plate that he had picked up from him.

He and Annabelle disappeared into the living room, and Mary cleaned the kitchen. Then, remembering what Nicole had said about Lucas liking quiet evenings and also the fact that she was now off duty, she went to her bedroom.

The next week flew by. Mary quickly learned that Annabelle didn't always want to follow the rules, and even the promise of another star didn't always work. So, with Lucas's permission, she had implemented the use of a time-out chair.

Thankfully, she didn't see much of her boss since he left before she got up in the mornings and came home at dinnertime. The less she was around him, the better—because she definitely had a huge crush on him.

Not only was he physically attractive, but he also was kind and had a fun sense of humor. She loved watching him interact with his daughter. He was so gentle and loving with her. He was exceedingly patient with her, too.

All those things only made him more attractive to Mary. Of course, he had been nothing but nice and respectful to her. Nothing would come of Mary's crush, as long as she didn't do or say anything stupid to him and ruin the harmony they had found in their working relationship.

She had to remember this was a job that also gave her a beautiful place to live. The last thing she would want to do was jeopardize that.

More importantly, she needed to remember what Nicole had told her—that Lucas had been broken by the fate that took his beloved wife away from him.

Because of the love he had for his wife, he would never marry again.

Mary found that tragically sad, both for him and the motherless little girl she was also growing to love.

Midmorning Saturday, Lucas walked down the hallway to Mary's room. So far, he was extremely pleased he had hired her. The evening meals had been delicious, and Annabelle appeared to be thriving under Mary's care.

The only thing he was vaguely surprised by was how much time she spent in her room. Every evening, after cleaning up the kitchen, she would disappear for the night.

He'd just assumed when he hired her that there would be evenings when they spent time together, even if it was just watching television. He'd sort of hoped for that kind of companionship, but it certainly wasn't her job to sit around and visit with him during his long, lonely evenings.

Her time was her own, and if she wanted to spend it alone in her room, then that was okay with him. However, it was midmorning on a Saturday, and despite her being off duty, he intended now to invite her out. If she decided to join him and Annabelle, then great. If she declined his offer, that was okay, too.

He knocked on her door; it took just a moment for her to open it. "Lucas, is something wrong?" she immediately asked.

"No, not at all. The heat has lessened a bit outside today, so I was wondering if you'd like to take a walk with me and Annabelle," he said. "We're just going around the property and down by the cornfield."

"Oh, I'd love to go," she replied.

"I suggest you put on a pair of jeans. You don't want to get chigger bites, and it might be a little dusty."

"Okay, I'll change and be right out."

Minutes later, she walked into the living room, clad in a pair of nice-fitting jeans and a short-sleeved green blouse that perfectly matched her eyes.

"Oh, Annabelle, I love your overalls," she said.

Annabelle preened. "I'm a farmer."

"That's right, peanut. You're a farmer just like your daddy," Lucas said as he picked her up. He was also wearing a pair of overalls; Annabelle always wanted to wear hers whenever he wore his. He grinned at Mary. "Ready to head out?"

Mary smiled. "Ready."

They left by the back door. He set Annabelle down, and she immediately reached for Lucas's hand and then for Mary's, and they headed across the backyard.

"It's a beautiful day," Mary said.

"Yeah, the weatherman says we're supposed to have several days of these milder temperatures, but then it gets hot again," he replied.

He couldn't help but notice the golden highlights that sparkled and shone in her hair. As usual, it was pulled back in a long braid down her back. He also couldn't help but wonder what it might look like down and around her shoulders.

He couldn't imagine why Nicole had mentioned Mary being plain. He didn't find her plain at all. Was she a raving beauty like Diana had been? No. But there were all kinds of beauty, and Mary was definitely a quiet kind of beauty.

"So, are you taking your online classes now?" he asked as they walked. Certainly, that would explain the amount of time she spent in her room. Maybe she was studying and taking tests.

"No, not right now," she replied. "I'm hoping to get back in for the fall semester."

"Have you always wanted to be a teacher?"

"Always. I've always wanted to work with young children. It's just taken me longer than most to get there. Working at the grocery store paid me enough for my living expenses, but I'd have to save up to take the courses, and I couldn't always afford the classes."

"You didn't want to take out a loan or didn't qualify for grants?" he asked curiously.

"I definitely didn't want to apply for a grant that somebody else might have needed more than me, and I definitely didn't want a loan. I want to finish up school not owing anyone anything."

"That's admirable," he replied. Annabelle had been walking quietly between them, but then she folded up her legs, forcing him and Mary to lift her up. She squealed and giggled as they carried her like that for several feet.

"Okay, that's enough, Annabelle. Put your feet down and walk like a big girl," he said. He breathed a sigh of relief when she complied.

"So, what do you enjoy doing in your spare time?" he asked Mary.

"There are several television shows I enjoy watching, and I also like to read."

"What TV shows do you like?" he asked.

She mentioned several that he also watched. "You should come out of your room in the evenings and watch them with me on the big-screen TV in the living room."

She shot him a quick look of surprise. "I thought you didn't like having anyone around you during the evenings."

It was his turn to look at her in surprise. "Where on earth did you get that idea?"

"Uh...Nicole told me you enjoy quiet evenings with nobody around."

"Daddy, pick me up?" Annabelle said. "My legs can't work anymore."

Lucas laughed and then picked up his daughter, who had obviously tired of walking. "I think Nicole was trying to protect me in case you were a chatty kind of woman."

She smiled at him. "Nobody has ever called me a chatty woman." She had a beautiful smile, one that showed her pretty white teeth and sparkled in her eyes and held an abundance of warmth.

"Good, then it's settled. You are welcome to hang

out with me in the evenings whenever you want to," he said.

"Only on one condition—you promise to tell me if and when you tire of my company. It won't hurt my feelings at all, and I won't take it personal."

"Deal," he replied.

They were now walking along the side of the cornfield. "Have you always raised corn?" she asked.

"Always. Like my father and his father before him."

"Is your father still around?" she asked.

"When I was eighteen years old, my father deeded this place and all the land to me, and then he left for California. He's now living on a houseboat and, according to him, he's living his best life."

"Then you were pretty young when you took over here," she observed.

"I was old enough to work hard in the fields, but I wasn't even old enough to get a beer at the Farmer's Club," he said jokingly.

The Farmer's Club was a bar/grill where a lot of the men and some women farmers around the area would go to visit with each other and have a few drinks.

It was a low-key kind of bar. There was a shuffleboard and darts. The place created a sense of community among the farmers, who were generally isolated in their work.

"Do you go to the Farmer's Club often?" she asked.

"I occasionally go on a Saturday night just to have

a beer or two and talk to the other men in the area about crops and weather and farmer stuff."

"'Farmer stuff,'" Annabelle echoed, as if to remind them she was there. "Daddy, piggyback."

Lucas moved his daughter from his arms to his shoulders, and she grabbed him tightly around his neck. "I love you, Daddy!" she exclaimed. "And I like Ms. Mary."

"I like you, too, Annabelle," Mary replied with another one of her sunshiny smiles. Her gaze left the little girl, and she glanced toward the cornstalks.

She suddenly froze, her entire body appearing to stiffen. One of her hands reached up and clapped over her mouth as if to stifle a scream, and the other hand pointed to a place in the corn.

He followed her finger, and he gasped when he saw what she did. There were various scarecrows placed inside the corn rows to keep the crows away, but the scarecrow he saw now filled him with horror.

It wasn't a straw-stuffed old shirt with a hat on top. Despite what had been done to her, he recognized the woman hanging on the stake. It was Cindy Perry, a cute waitress from the café in town.

Only she wasn't cute now. Her mouth had been sewn together with thick black thread, and her eyes were missing, as if pecked out by crows. It was a nightmarish sight that had him momentarily frozen in shock.

"Come on, Annabelle. Let's go back to the house

and play a game," Mary said, her voice high and breathless.

"What kind of a game?" Annabelle asked as Lucas quickly set her on the ground.

Lucas was grateful when Mary grabbed her hand and pulled her in the direction of the house. "We'll decide what game on the way back to the house."

He watched them go, and once they were gone, he turned back around to take in the horrible sight. Cindy was clad in a pair of ragged jeans and a long-sleeved red-and-black plaid shirt. A straw hat sat on her head at a cocky angle.

The horror of the sewn-up lips and the missing eyes sent a shudder straight through him. What the hell? Who had done this heinous thing? Who had killed Cindy? And who had made her into a human scarecrow? It was evil and vile.

He finally got his wits about him enough to pull his cell phone out of his pocket. He punched in the number of the man who was not only one of his good friends but also the chief of police for Millsville.

Dallas Calloway answered on the second ring. "Dallas, it's Lucas. I have a situation here," Lucas said.

"What kind of a situation?"

"You need to call Josiah Mills and meet me at my place." Josiah was the coroner.

There was a long pause. "Is it Nicole?"

"No, it's Cindy Perry, and she's been murdered and left in my cornfield," Lucas replied.

"On my way." Dallas hung up.

Lucas put his phone away. No matter how much he didn't want to look, his gaze was drawn again and again to Cindy. She had been a cute young woman. Even now in death, the short blond hair that peeked out from under the hat sparkled in the sunlight. Her eyes had been a bright blue—oh, God, what had happened to her eyes?

Thank God Mary had responded quickly and gotten Annabelle out of here before the little girl had seen this horror. Annabelle was fine, but what about Mary?

She had to be feeling the same way he was: sick to her stomach, horrified by the scene and wondering who was responsible for this obscene murder. Hell, for all he knew, she might be packing her bags right now.

He finally walked back toward the house, where he stood out front to wait for Dallas. His brain whirled dizzily with questions. Thankfully, Dallas's cop car pulled up within minutes.

The tall dark-haired man got out of the vehicle and approached Lucas. "Hey, man," he said in greeting. "I got in touch with Josiah, and he should be here in about a half an hour or so." Josiah Mills was far past retirement age but had continued to work in his position.

"She's in the cornfield. You want to take a look before anyone else gets here?" Lucas asked.

"Definitely."

Together the two men headed back to where the human scarecrow was located. "Do you know how long she's been out here?" Dallas asked.

"No more than two days. I was out in this area day before yesterday, and she wasn't here," Lucas replied.

When Dallas saw her, he gasped and stumbled back a couple of steps. "Damn, man. You should have warned me," he said as he stared at Cindy. "You have any idea why she was left here in your cornfield?"

"Not a clue."

"I need to call in some more men to process the scene, although that's going to be difficult with it being in the middle of the corn," Dallas said. "We need to wait for Josiah to tell us more." Dallas's gray eyes darkened. "I can't believe somebody did this to her. Damn—do you think the crows took her eyes out?"

"Maybe. I guess Josiah will be able to tell us for sure," Lucas replied, his stomach churning at the thought.

An hour and a half later, all the photos had been taken and a preliminary search around the area had been conducted. Josiah and his assistant, Gary Walters, cut Cindy down with the help of several other officers who had arrived and placed her on a tarp next to the corn rows.

An hour after that, Josiah was finished with his initial examination. He straightened from the body and put both hands on his slender back. "I'm getting too damn old for this," he said with a cranky growl.

"So, what can you tell me?" Dallas asked.

"It appears cause of death is five knife wounds to the chest. Time of death I would set at sometime yesterday between the hours of noon and five. Obviously, the death occurred elsewhere, and she was staged here afterward." Josiah spoke matter-of-factly and without any emotion in his voice.

"What about her eyes?" Lucas couldn't help but ask.

"From my preliminary observation, I believe the eyes were removed with a knife or a scalpel, not pecked out by any birds." Josiah looked at his assistant. "Gary, let's get her on a stretcher and loaded up. I'll be able to tell you more once I get her on the table in the morgue," he added to Dallas. "If anything I said out here proves incorrect, I'll call you."

Minutes later, Cindy's body was gone, taken to the morgue for further examination and tests. "I'll be up at the house, if you need me," Lucas finally said to Dallas. He knew the officers would go through the scene with a fine-tooth comb, and there was really nothing more he could do.

When he entered the house, it was quiet. Mary was seated on the sofa, but she stood when he walked in. "I fed Annabelle lunch and then put her down for a nap."

"Thanks." He motioned for her to sit back down before joining her on the sofa. "And thanks for getting her out of there so fast."

"I didn't want that vision in her head," she replied.

However, it was obvious by the paleness of her face and the darkness of her eyes that the vision of Cindy the scarecrow was very much in her head. "What did Dallas have to say?"

"Not much, other than he'd be up to talk to us later." He could smell Mary's scent—a soft lilac that momentarily overtook the stench of death in his head.

She wrapped her arms around her waist, as if suddenly cold and needing to warm herself. "I certainly don't know anything about this. I didn't even know Cindy, other than she occasionally waited on me when I ate at the café."

He had the oddest desire to pull her close to warm her, to soothe her. It was bizarre. In truth, he still didn't know her very well. She'd been his employee for a week, and a dead woman had shown up in his cornfield.

He couldn't help but wonder if something in her past had caused this to happen. Did Mary know more than she was telling? Whom had he invited into his life? More importantly, whom had he invited into his daughter's life?

Chapter 4

Mary couldn't get the awful picture of Cindy out of her head. Dear God, who had done such a heinous thing? It was positively evil. Out of all the cornfields in the county, why had Cindy's body been left in Lucas's?

A million questions swirled around in her head when Dallas showed up an hour later to talk to them. He got right to the point. "Mary, have you ever had problems with Cindy before?" he asked, his gray eyes on her, dark and intense.

"No, not at all," she replied. "I told Lucas a little while ago—I didn't even know her other than she waited on me a couple of times at the café."

"Same with me," Lucas added. "I really didn't know her at all."

"Do either of you know if anyone had a problem with her?"

Both she and Lucas answered negatively.

Dallas frowned. "Lucas, why your cornfield?"

"Hell if I know," Lucas replied fervently. He leaned forward on the sofa. "Dallas, we've been friends since we were kids. You've got to believe I had absolutely nothing to do with this. I don't know who did this or why she was left in my cornfield."

"And I would hope nobody in my life could be responsible for something so horrible like this." A cold chill shot up Mary's spine.

"In a town this size, we probably all know the killer," Dallas said grimly.

"That's horrifying in and of itself," she said. "It's shocking that a murder has occurred, but what was done to her was positively vile." She fought against the new shiver that threatened to walk up her spine.

"Speaking of what was done to her... I'd like to keep the details of her death and how she was found as close to the chest as possible. That means I need you two to keep them close to your chests as well. Please don't gossip about what you've seen. It would interfere with the investigation."

"I've never been a gossiper, and I certainly don't intend to become one now," Mary said. "Especially about this."

"Same with me," Lucas replied.

Dallas nodded. "Whoever it is, I'm going to find this killer and make sure he or she is put behind bars so this can't happen to anyone else." Dallas stood up from his chair.

"Do you really think this could happen again?" Lucas asked.

"I can't dismiss anything—but I sure as hell hope this is a single horrifying murder specific to something that was going on in Cindy's life."

"I'll walk you out," Lucas said and rose from the sofa.

As the two men left, Mary sat back and drew in several deep, long breaths. She felt as if she hadn't caught her breath since she'd stifled her scream at the first sight of Cindy.

This all was a horrible nightmare. It was going to take her a very long time to get the vision of Cindy on that stake out of her head. She was so grateful Annabelle hadn't seen her. Mary only hoped the sight of Cindy didn't invade her own sleep in the form of nightmares.

She looked up when Lucas came back in. He sank down on the sofa next to her and released a deep breath. "To be honest with you, I was afraid you'd be packing your bags to leave by now," he said. "But I swear to you, Mary—I had nothing to do with this, and I have no idea why she was left in my cornfield."

He looked so earnest. His gaze exuded an honesty and innocence that she desperately wanted to believe. Besides, it was hard for her to imagine that he could lovingly tuck in his daughter and then go out and not only murder Cindy but also truss her up like a human scarecrow.

"I don't know you very well, Lucas. But what I know of you, I can't imagine you having anything to do with this."

"Thank you," he replied with obvious relief. "And thank you for not immediately packing your bags and leaving us."

"You may ask me to do that after tasting more of my meals," she replied in an effort to lighten the mood a bit.

He let out a quick laugh and then smiled at her. "Thanks. I needed that."

"So, what happens now?" she asked, returning to soberness.

"I've never been a part of anything like this before, but I'm assuming Dallas will be questioning the people in Cindy's personal life and her coworkers at the café."

"I hope he finds this person quickly," she said, fighting another shiver.

"That makes two of us," he replied.

"It's just hard to believe somebody we know could be capable of something like this. I mean, why do that to her? And as terrible as this sounds, I hope it was done to her after her death."

"I know what you mean, and I share the same sentiment. I hope like hell she wasn't alive when she was…was…so defiled."

Annabelle came running out of her bedroom,

smiling and happy after her nap, as always. When Lucas began to play with his daughter, Mary went back to her own bedroom.

She tried to busy herself by playing some games on her computer in an effort to get the vision of Cindy out of her brain. When that didn't work, she grabbed the book she'd been reading off her nightstand, hoping the lighthearted romantic comedy would provide a little escape from murder and horrifying scarecrows.

Lucas made hamburgers and french fries for dinner. The three of them ate together, and the talk between them remained benign and easy. Once they had finished eating, Mary helped with the cleanup and then returned to her room.

It was right before seven when a knock fell on her door. It was Lucas. "Want to come out and watch some television with me?"

"Sure, I'd like that," she agreed. She was looking for any distraction from the dark thoughts of murder that refused to leave her head.

In the living room, he sat down in his recliner, and she curled up in a corner of the sofa. Annabelle was already in bed for the night. He turned on a crime show that Mary had told him she watched. Apparently, he watched it, too, for at every commercial break, they talked about old plotlines and the changes and growth in the characters.

This was a pattern that played out over the next five days as their routine became more established.

Only Annabelle now insisted each evening that Mary tuck her into bed for the night as well as her daddy.

Dallas had not been back to talk to them about Cindy's murder, which indicated the investigation had moved away from them. They still had no clue why Cindy had been in Lucas's cornfield. It had taken several days for officers to finish processing the scene in the cornfield, but now they were gone.

Nicole had dropped by several times in the early evenings and had told Mary and Lucas the murder was still a hot topic of conversation and speculation in town. At least now Mary could get through a day without thinking about Cindy's death.

With each day that passed, Mary's crush on her boss went deeper and deeper. The more time she spent around him, the more she liked him. In the past, she had spent a lot of time thinking about what kind of man she'd like to marry one day.

He'd have to be kind and smart. He would need to love children and have a good sense of humor. He would also need to respect and encourage her desire to teach school. Lucas checked all the boxes she'd ever had for the kind of man she could fall in love with.

Unfortunately, he was her boss, and she couldn't cross that line with him—not that he'd indicated he wanted to cross that line with her. Still, that didn't stop her from crushing on him hard.

It was Thursday night, and Mary had once again settled on the sofa to watch television with Lucas.

She'd come to believe over the past few days that her employer was a lonely man. He might cling tightly to the memory of his wife, but a dead woman couldn't fill the silent hours of a long evening.

"Tell me about your parents, Mary," he said just before the show started. "I know they live here in town, but I've never heard you mention anything about them, and you don't go visit them."

She frowned and fought against the hurt that thoughts of her parents always brought with them. "We aren't very close. To be perfectly honest, I don't believe they wanted any children, and I think I was probably a mistake...an accident. They were cold and distant with me for as long as I can remember. They didn't spend any time with me or tuck me in at night. The only time they showed any real warmth to me was on my eighteenth birthday when they gifted me two suitcases and my car, and told me to move out."

The warmth of a blush rose up in her cheeks. "I'm sorry. I'm sure that was far more information than you wanted."

"Please, don't apologize. I'm just sorry you had that kind of a childhood," he replied. His gaze was soft, and for a moment, she wanted to fall into the beautiful blue depths and lose herself there.

A knock sounded on the front door. "Sit tight," Lucas said as he got out of his chair.

A moment later, Celeste Winthrop walked in with a covered plate and Lucas just behind her. She stopped short, obviously surprised to see Mary.

Celeste turned back to Lucas. "Oh, I didn't know you already had company."

"Mary isn't company. She's my live-in nanny and housekeeper," Lucas replied.

"Hello, Celeste," Mary said.

"Mary," Celeste replied with a rigid nod of her head.

Celeste was an attractive woman with ash-blond hair and brown eyes. She was a divorcée who had rarely acknowledged Mary whenever she had rung her up at the grocery store. Now she narrowed her eyes at Mary and then turned back to Lucas with a bright smile.

"I baked cookies today for the garden club, and I just happened to bake some extras, knowing how much Annabelle loves my chocolate chip ones." She offered him the plate.

"Thank you, Celeste," Lucas said. "That was too kind of you."

Mary got up from the sofa. "I'll carry those into the kitchen."

"Thank you, Mary," Lucas said as she took the plate from him.

She carried the cookies into the kitchen and placed them on the counter, then headed to her bedroom. She assumed Celeste would stay and visit. It was obvious she had designs on Lucas, and Mary suspected the way to Lucas's heart was definitely to do nice things for his daughter.

She was about to change into her nightshirt when

Lucas knocked on her door. "I paused the TV show, so do you want to come back out and finish it?"

"Oh, I just assumed you and Celeste would be visiting," she said.

"I didn't invite her to sit down and visit," he replied.

"Then I'd love to finish the program with you."

Minutes later, they were back in their places, watching the show. When a commercial came on, he paused it. "You know, I'm not a dumb man," he said.

"I never thought you were," Mary replied, surprised by his statement.

"I'm aware that Celeste and several other women in town have set their sights on me as an eligible bachelor. I know they're courting me with casseroles and cookies and whatever." A deep frown cut across his forehead.

"I've tried to discourage them—but by Celeste's visit tonight, I obviously need to be firmer and let them know in no uncertain terms that I'm not interested in getting remarried. I had my great love with Diana, and when she died, my heart closed up forever."

He flushed and raked a hand through his hair. "Sorry, I didn't mean to bore you with all that. I guess chocolate chip cookies somehow trigger me," he finished with a grin.

She laughed. "For me, it's brussels sprouts."

"Brussels sprouts?" He looked at her in amusement.

She nodded. "My parents forced me to eat them

when I was little and they believed I had been bad. I hated them. I still hate them to this day and have always felt like eating them is a punishment."

It was his turn to laugh. "Then I guess I shouldn't plan on brussels sprouts being on the evening menu anytime soon."

God, she loved the sound of his laughter. It was deep and full-bodied and made her smile every time she heard it. "Not unless you love them. Only then will I cook them."

"You definitely don't have to cook them for me," he replied. "There are lots of other vegetables without having to ever eat a brussels sprout for the rest of our lives."

The rest of the evening passed pleasantly. Later that night, as she got ready for bed, she replayed his words about the death of his wife and the closure of his heart forever.

It was tragically sad to her that a man she suspected had a lot of love in his heart to give had decided to be buried along with his wife.

Even if he never looked at her as anything but his daughter's nanny, she hoped he would one day open his heart enough to love again—not only for his sake but for Annabelle's sake as well.

Lucas was out of her league. It was ridiculous to even think he might be attracted to a woman like her. His wife had been utterly gorgeous, and Mary knew she was a bit of a plain Jane. Come fall, she needed to stay focused on her job and on her schooling. And she also needed to recognize that love might never be in the cards for her.

It was another Saturday morning, and Lucas, Mary and Annabelle were seated at the kitchen table, enjoying the pancakes and bacon Lucas had made for breakfast.

Lucas was in a great mood after another week of the household running like a well-oiled machine with Mary in charge. The evening meals had been delicious, and after being rewarded ten stars for good behavior and helping out, Annabelle had earned a new baby doll.

He tried not to think about poor Cindy. It was still disturbing to think of her left in his cornfield, but he didn't want thoughts of her to take away the personal peace he was finding in his life.

"There's nothing better than bacon and maple syrup," Mary said.

"Unless it's beer and barbecue," he replied.

"Or potato chips and mayo."

"Really?" One of his dark brows rose up.

"Really. You should try them together some time."

He laughed. "I might just do that. What else do you like to eat?"

"Mashed 'tatoes," Annabelle said. "And mac and cheese."

"Yes, I know how much you like mac and cheese," Mary said to Annabelle. She looked at Lucas. "Almost every day she asks for mac and cheese for lunch."

"Does she get it every day?" Lucas asked.

"Heavens, no." Mary laughed. "She gets it maybe once a week or so, and it comes with vegetables."

"Vegetables make me strong," Annabelle quipped and bent her arm to display an invisible muscle.

"That's right," Lucas agreed with a grin. How things had changed since Mary had been here. Annabelle had refused to eat vegetables before; now his daughter didn't seem to mind eating healthier.

A knock sounded at the front door. Lucas got up to answer and, moments later, came back in the room with Nicole. "Doesn't this look nice," she said.

"Granny, did you bring me a present?" Annabelle asked.

"Annabelle, what did we talk about?" Mary asked.

"I not 'posed to ask for presents," Annabelle said solemnly and then looked back at Mary, who nodded and smiled.

"That's very good, Annabelle, but this morning I did bring you a present," Nicole said. She pulled a baby doll outfit out of her oversize purse. "It's pajamas for one of your babies. I'll just set them here on the counter because it looks like you have sticky syrup fingers right now."

"What do you say, Annabelle?" Lucas asked.

"Thank you, Granny," she said, beaming brightly at Nicole. "I'm going to put it on baby Annie. She's always naked."

Nicole laughed. "Then I'm glad I brought her some clothes."

"Nicole, would you like some pancakes?" Lucas asked. "I can easily put another plate on the table."

"No, thanks, although I wouldn't mind a cup of coffee," she replied as she sat in an empty chair at the table. She looked nice in a pair of black slacks and a rosy pink blouse that enhanced her dark hair and blue eyes.

"Mary, it looks like you've settled in quite nicely," she said with a pleasant smile.

"I don't know what I'd do without her," Lucas replied.

"Well, Annabelle and Lucas both appear happy, so you must be doing something right," Nicole replied.

"I hope so. We seem to have established a good routine that's working for everyone," Mary said.

"I happy, Granny. I happy." Annabelle smiled broadly at Nicole.

Nicole laughed. "I'm glad to hear that, my little cupcake." She sobered as Lucas set a cup of coffee before her and then returned to his own seat. "Thank goodness Dallas's investigation has moved away from here."

"Yeah, he moved on pretty quickly, although I haven't heard much more about the investigation. Except the little bits and pieces you've told me that you've heard in town," Lucas replied. "I haven't even been in town for the last couple of weeks."

"And I've only been to town once to pick up some groceries and a reward for Annabelle," Mary said.

"I got ten stars, Granny," Annabelle said proudly. "I got ten stars, and Ms. Mary got me a 'ward. It was a new baby doll."

Mary quickly explained the star system to Nicole. "That's wonderful that you got ten stars, Annabelle." Nicole reached over and patted her granddaughter's arm.

"Daddy, can I get down?"

"Let's wash those sticky fingers first," Mary said.

Lucas watched as Mary got up, wet a paper towel and then proceeded to wash his daughter's face and hands.

Today Mary was once again wearing jeans that hugged her long legs and showed off her slender waist. Her bright yellow short-sleeved blouse did amazing things to her green eyes.

Although the smell of bacon and syrup filled his head right now, he knew if he leaned closer to her, he would catch the scent of spring flowers…heavy on the lilac. It was a scent he'd grown to love.

When Annabelle left the room, Lucas once again turned his attention to his mother-in-law. "What have you heard about Cindy's murder investigation?"

Nicole took a sip of her coffee before replying. "Initially, everyone was buzzing about the news, and I know Dallas conducted all kinds of interviews at the café. But the news now is that the investigation has stalled, and Dallas has no real suspects."

She shook her head and wrapped her fingers around her coffee cup. "I haven't asked you two any questions, but it must have been horrifying for you to find her like that."

"What do you mean, 'like that'? What have you heard about her?" Lucas asked.

"I heard she was made into a human scarecrow— that her eyes had been pecked out by the birds, and there were cuts on her face sewn up with thick black thread," Nicole replied.

Lucas looked at Mary and then back at Nicole in surprise. "Dallas wanted to keep much of that away from the general public." Even though the description wasn't quite right, it was close enough.

"Somehow, it leaked out." Nicole shrugged. "Anyway, she must have been a horrible sight."

"I still have nightmares about it," Mary admitted.

Lucas looked at her in surprise. He hated that she was having nightmares about Cindy, although he really shouldn't be surprised. It had been a heinous sight and would have given most people nightmares.

Nicole visited for another few minutes and then left. "Stop. Remember, this is your day off," he said to Mary, who had gotten up from the table and grabbed plates to clear.

She laughed. "You cooked, so I don't mind helping clean up."

"So, do you have any big plans for today?" he asked before she could head back to her room.

"Actually, I do. I'm meeting Sally Roth this evening for dinner at the café."

"That will be nice for you…an evening away from me and my kid. And Sally seems like a nice young woman." Sally had rung him up at the grocery store many times in the past.

"Right, I can't wait to get away from you and Annabelle," she said with a teasing light in her eyes. "I plan on lingering over dinner and dessert, so hopefully you'll be in bed when I get home, and I won't have to see your ugly mug for the rest of the night."

He laughed, delighted that she felt comfortable enough to joke with him. "I'll try to head to bed early just to accommodate you."

"Thanks, I would appreciate that," she replied with a playful smile. Together they finished cleaning up the kitchen, and then she headed back to her room.

His smile stayed on his face for a long time. Minutes later, he was playing baby dolls with his daughter, thinking again of how grateful he was that he'd hired Mary. He seemed to be smiling a lot lately.

"Daddy, come play some more," Annabelle said a half an hour later as she ran out of her room and into the living room, where he had just sat down.

He stood. "How about I bring your blocks in here, and we can build big towers?" he suggested.

"'Kay," she agreed. "Big, big towers."

Minutes later, he was on the floor with Annabelle. It was the usual game: he'd build the towers, and then she would knock them down and giggle.

He loved the sound of her laughter. She was the single greatest thing he would ever accomplish in his lifetime. After just three weeks, he could see the progress Mary had made with Annabelle. His daughter was listening more and throwing fewer temper tantrums. She loved earning her stars and did not like time-out, where Mary made her sit in a chair for three long minutes.

He'd just made five tall towers to be knocked down when a rap fell on the front door. When he opened it, Gina Hightower smiled at him brightly, holding a stewpot in one arm. She quickly offered it to him.

"I had some family over to eat last night, and I made far too much spaghetti and too many meatballs, so I thought you and Annabelle might enjoy eating the leftovers," she said.

"I like sketti," Annabelle chirped from just behind Lucas.

"Hi, Annabelle. How are you doing, sweetheart?" Gina leaned down and smiled at her.

"Daddy and I are playing," she said.

"That's nice. Maybe sometime I can come over and play with you," Gina replied.

Lucas couldn't imagine the dark-haired, well-dressed woman ever getting down on the floor to play with Annabelle. Gina struck him as someone who wouldn't want her hair to get mussed or her clothes to get wrinkled.

She was unlike Mary, who rolled around on the

floor with Annabelle, not caring if her clothes got dirty or her hair got messy.

"Gina, you have to stop bringing us food," he said. "While I appreciate your kindness, it's completely unnecessary." What he wanted to say was that no matter how many meals or goodies she brought him, he wasn't going to marry her. Heck, he didn't even want to date her. She was a nice lady, but he wasn't— and would never be—involved romantically with her.

However, saying such things to her at this moment would only make things awkward, especially in front of Annabelle. He didn't want his little girl to hear a grown-up conversation like that.

"Lucas, I really don't mind bringing things to you. I can't imagine what it's like to be a single working father. It must be so difficult, and you must always be juggling things," she replied.

"Actually, things have been running quite smoothly around here since three weeks ago, when I hired Mary Curtis to be my live-in nanny and housekeeper. She's been absolutely wonderful."

"Mary Curtis? Oh, you mean Mary from the grocery store. I didn't know you'd hired her," Gina replied with a raised eyebrow. "So she's living here with you?"

"Yes, she lives here," Lucas said.

"Ms. Mary plays with me," Annabelle said.

"That's nice," Gina replied, but her tone was a tad bit cooler than it had been moments before. She looked back at Lucas. "Well, I hope you enjoy the spaghetti. I'll swing by some evening in the next week or so to get my pot back."

With a murmured goodbye, she was gone. Lucas closed the door after her with a wry grin. Apparently, having Mary living here had the unexpected benefit of chasing women away. That definitely wasn't a bad thing.

He carried the pot of spaghetti into the kitchen and made room for it in the refrigerator. He had a feeling this would be the last thing Gina brought him—and that was fine.

It was just after six when Mary came out of her room. She was wearing a pink-and-white-striped sundress. The scoop neck hinted at her cleavage, and the short dress showcased her shapely legs. Her shiny hair was loose, cascading over her shoulders and down her back. She looked positively charming.

His fingers suddenly itched with the need to run them through her long hair. If he got close enough, would he smell her scent emanating from the base of her throat? From between her breasts? Would her eyes darken with pleasure if he leaned in for a kiss?

For the first time in years, a swift, hot desire punched him in the gut. It was completely unexpected and more than a bit of a shock. But it was there only a moment—and then gone.

"You look very nice," he finally managed to say.

"Thank you. Well, I'm off. I'll be home later."

"Enjoy your dinner." He walked her to the front door.

"Thanks, I will. I always enjoy spending time with Sally," she replied. "She can be so funny."

"Then I'll see you later," he replied.

A moment later, she was gone. It was strange—she'd only been in his home for the last three weeks, but the house felt oddly empty without her in it.

He realized he would miss her this evening. He'd gotten used to watching television with her and talking to her. He thought back to that moment when he'd felt that sudden desire for Mary.

He supposed he shouldn't be too surprised; he hadn't been with a woman in years. It was probably only natural that his testosterone would reawaken again after so long, especially since he found Mary to be an attractive woman.

However, there was no place for those kinds of feelings where Mary was concerned. The last thing he wanted to do was ruin the good, easy working relationship they were building. Mary was the perfect nanny and live-in help. He admired and respected her. He would never follow through on any desire for her he might entertain, especially knowing his heart could never be open again.

Chapter 5

As Mary drove to the café to meet Sally for dinner, her thoughts were still filled with the man she had just left. While she'd been in her room getting ready for the evening out, she'd heard a woman's voice in the living room.

Lucas was definitely one hot commodity in this small town. She certainly understood why. If Mary was looking for a potential husband, Lucas would definitely be at the top of the list.

However, Mary wasn't in the market for a husband. What she needed was to get her life together. She needed to finish her schooling and get her teaching degree, and then she wanted to be hired on as a teacher at Millsville Elementary. That way, she could always take care of herself, maybe eventually buy a small home of her own and start building a pension.

If a man happened to come along at any time in that process—a man who supported her career choices and loved her desperately and madly, a man she loved desperately and madly, too—she'd be all in.

But at twenty-eight years old, she'd never had a man who loved her desperately and madly, and she wasn't expecting one to suddenly pop up now.

She'd thought she had met a decent and respectable man on the dating site, but it hadn't taken long before Kenny Majors had turned on her and become her cyberterrorizer. Thank goodness he lived hundreds of miles away and had no idea where she was now living.

Thoughts of men and marriage all left her head as she approached the café and anticipated spending time with Sally. Since it was a Saturday evening, the place was packed, and she had to park a block away.

The weather had turned cloudy, bringing a twilight darkness that was unusual so early in the night. She hurried down the sidewalk, hoping the cloudy skies didn't mean rain. Although, as dry and hot as it had been, she imagined the farmers in the area wouldn't mind a night of soil-soaking rain.

She pulled open the café door. Immediately, a variety of scents filled her head that made her stomach growl with hunger. Frying onions and simmering meat, baking bread and other pleasant smells swirled around her.

The café was colorful, with bright yellow hay bales and red roosters painted on one wall. A cornfield was painted on another wall, and a patchwork of farmland in greens, golds and brown was on the third wall. She scanned the tables and booths to see if Sally had already arrived.

Not seeing her friend, she made her way to an empty two-top table toward the back. As she walked past the other tables, several people she knew from the grocery store offered her pleasant smiles. She took a seat facing the front door, and a moment later, Sally walked into the café.

Sally had medium brown hair cut in a style that framed her gamin features. Tonight, she was dressed in a cute blue sundress that showed off her petite frame.

Mary waved at her and smiled as Sally spied her and hurried toward their table. "Hey, girl, it's been a while," Sally said as she dropped into the chair opposite Mary.

"It does feel like a long time," Mary agreed. "So, tell me what's new at the grocery store."

Before they could chat, the waitress arrived to take their orders. Sally ordered a burger and fries, while Mary opted for the special: meat loaf and mashed potatoes.

Once the waitress had served their drinks, Sally filled Mary in on all the happenings at the grocery store. "The big news is that Samantha finally got engaged to Brian."

"Oh, good for them," Mary replied. Samantha Lindsay had worked at the grocery store for four years, and she and Brian Lanfield had been dating for over five.

"Yeah, she's really happy that he finally proposed. They plan on getting married sometime next year. She said it would just be a small ceremony. Now, forget about the grocery store," Sally said. She tucked a strand of hair behind her ear and leaned forward, her blue eyes sparkling brightly. "I want to hear all about you. I can't believe you're actually living with hunky Lucas Maddox. He makes me half-breathless when I check him out at the grocery store. I want to hear positively everything."

Mary laughed. "I'm afraid you're going to be bored to death."

"I'm guessing, then, that you haven't slept with him yet."

"Oh, Sally, gosh, no." A flaming blush filled Mary's cheeks.

Sally grinned. "But that blush tells me there's something going on. Spill the beans."

"Really, there's nothing at all to tell. It is a great job, but I only see him in the evenings. I spend my days with his daughter. I clean and cook dinner for them each night."

"What's he like behind closed doors?" Sally asked. "He always seems really nice when he's in the store."

"He's just as nice behind closed doors. He's kind and respectful and has a great sense of humor. He's a wonderful, loving father, and it warms my heart to see him interact with Annabelle."

Sally stared at her for a long moment. "You're absolutely crazy about him."

Mary laughed again. "I...I kind of am," she finally admitted. She was saved from saying anything more by the arrival of their orders.

However, Sally was tenacious. "So does he know how you feel about him?" she asked the moment the waitress left their table.

"Heavens, no," Mary replied, horrified at the very thought. "I like my job, and I'd never do anything to jeopardize it. Besides, he loved his wife so much he never wants to be in a relationship or marry again."

Sally sighed. "Gosh, I wish I could find a man who loved me that much." She paused a moment and then asked, "Have you seen him naked yet?"

Mary nearly choked on her soda. "Absolutely not," she finally managed to say. "Good grief, Sally."

Sally grinned naughtily. "I was just curious. I'll bet he's as hot naked as he is clothed."

Mary chuckled. "You are silly. Now, let's talk about your love life. Are you dating anyone right now?" Mary asked, hoping for a change in topic from a naked Lucas.

As they ate their meal, Sally talked about her dating life, making Mary laugh again and again. Sally definitely had a flair for the dramatic, and she had a wicked sense of humor that always tickled Mary.

However, their talk took a somber turn as they lingered over coffee. "So, were you there when they discovered Cindy in the cornfield?" Sally asked.

Mary nodded, instantly taken back to that horrible day. She could vividly remember the musty scent of the corn combined with the smell of rich, dark earth. The sky overhead had been a blue that was breathtakingly beautiful, and she'd been so pleased that he had invited her to take a walk with him.

"I heard she'd been made into a human scarecrow," Sally said, her voice lowered to a near-whisper.

"Where did you hear that?" Mary asked, remembering that Dallas had wanted to keep a lot of the information away from the general public.

"I heard that from Minnie Perkins. I was ringing her up at the grocery store, and she told me that Cindy was on a pole in the cornfield, and her lips had been sewn together and her eyes had been pecked out by birds."

"You know Minnie is a big gossiper, and you can't believe half of what she says," Mary replied.

"Yeah, but you were there. So is Minnie telling the truth?" Sally's gaze held hers intently.

Mary sighed inwardly. She didn't want to lie to her friend, but she also didn't want to add to any gossip that might interfere with the case. "I only saw her for a second. Annabelle was with us when we found her, so I quickly turned away, grabbed Annabelle and went back into the house. All I know is she was on a pole, posed like a scarecrow. I don't know anything else. I never heard any more about what was done to her," Mary replied.

"If I'd seen something like that, I think I would have packed my bags and gotten on the next plane bound for anywhere," Sally said. "Weren't you afraid to stay there with Lucas?"

"You know, it's funny—even though I didn't know him very well at that time, it never really entered my mind that Lucas might have had anything to do with the murder."

"Still, it's got to be scary to live in a place where a murder victim was found," Sally said.

"I try not to think about it," Mary said. It was true… Except for the occasional nightmares she had of scarecrows chasing her through a dark cornfield, she consciously didn't think about the murder.

It was almost eight when the two parted ways just outside the café. Darkness had completely fallen, and the smell of rain was in the air.

Mary hurried to her car, parked in the distance. She wanted to get home and settled in before the rain fell. Lightning filled the sky, backlighting the clouds in the distance.

She unlocked her car and slid in behind the steering wheel. It was only then that she saw it: some kind of flyer beneath her windshield wiper, effectively blocking her view out the front window.

Probably some sale advertisement from one of

the stores on Main Street, she thought as she opened the driver's-side door and stepped out to grab the piece of paper.

Once she was back in the car, she used the light from the dashboard to read the paper. LEAVE LUCAS'S HOUSE NOW OR FACE THE CONSEQUENCES. YOU'VE BEEN WARNED.

The bold red letters shot an icy chill up her spine. She quickly locked her doors and looked around. Who had left this…this threat for her? There were several people on the streets, but nobody appeared to be paying any attention to her.

She folded the note and put it in her purse, then started her car and pulled away from the curb. She was eager to get back as fear torched through her. Who wanted her out of Lucas's house and why? She was just a nanny who cared for his daughter and cleaned and cooked for him.

What consequences did the person who wrote the note mean? She tightened her grip on the steering wheel. *You've been warned.* The words echoed in her brain. What did that even mean? Why would she be warned to leave Lucas's house?

Even if she was frightened enough to immediately pack her bags and leave Lucas's house, she had no-where to go. Lucas and Annabelle were happy with her, and she was happy where she was. Who would feel threatened by that?

She finally reached Lucas's house and parked her car in her usual place along the side, then got out.

Her gaze shot left and right as she hurried through the dark to the front door.

When she walked into the living room, Annabelle ran toward her. "Ms. Mary. You're home!"

"Annabelle, what are you still doing up?" The little girl was in her pajamas, and it was way past her bedtime.

Lucas got up from the sofa and smiled at her. "She refused to go to bed until you tucked her in. I finally agreed to let her stay up a little longer to see if you'd get home before I absolutely insisted she go down."

Mary set her purse on the end table. "Come on, Annabelle. Let's go tuck you in right now. Us girls need to get our beauty sleep."

"Yeah, buty sleep," Annabelle agreed. She grabbed Mary's hand and yawned sleepily.

Annabelle's room was a little girl's dream. It was decorated in pink and lace, with enough toys to fill a store. Mary led her to the toddler bed, and Annabelle immediately crawled beneath the princess-decorated covers. It was obvious the child was beyond tired.

Mary pulled the sheet up beneath Annabelle's chin and then began to stroke the side of her face and across her little forehead. "The sleep fairies are coming to give you happy dreams," Mary whispered softly.

"I love sleep fairies," Annabelle said with a drowsy smile.

"I know you do. The fairies bring us wonderful dreams," Mary replied.

"Kiss me good-night?" Annabelle asked.

Mary leaned over and kissed the little girl's cheek. "There you go—a kiss to send you to sweet-dream land."

"Ms. Mary, I love you," Annabelle murmured, and then, with a tremulous sigh, she fell asleep.

It was the first time Annabelle had said those words to her, and they shot straight through to Mary's heart. She realized at that moment that she had grown to love the motherless child, too. It was going to take a heck of a lot more than an anonymous threatening note to make Mary walk away from Annabelle.

She left the bedroom and went back into the living room, where Lucas was seated on the sofa. "I tried to get her into bed half a dozen times before now, but she insisted she wasn't going to go to sleep until you were here to tuck her in."

"She's sleeping now." Mary grabbed her purse from the end table and sat down on the other side of the sofa. "You're lucky she doesn't mind naps or bedtime."

"She's always been like that," he replied. "Did you have a good time this evening?" he asked.

"I always have a good time with Sally. She can be a real hoot." Even as Mary said the words, her thoughts were on the threatening note in her purse.

Lucas gazed at her intently. "You don't look like you had a good time. Is something wrong?"

Mary flushed. She was surprised he'd picked up

on her mood. "Something happened when I left the café that was a bit disturbing."

Lucas leaned forward. "What do you mean? Disturbing how?"

She reached into her purse, withdrew the note and, after a moment of hesitation, handed it to him. A frown cut across his forehead as he took it from her and opened it. He read it, and then his gaze cut to her once again.

"What is this? Where did you find this?"

"It was under my windshield wiper on my car when I left the café to come home."

"Did you see who left it for you?" Concern deepened his voice.

"No, I don't have a clue who left it." She wrapped her arms around her waist to fight against the chill that threatened to wash over her.

"We need to call Dallas. He needs to see this," Lucas said.

"He won't be able to do anything about it," she said dispiritedly. "Whoever left it was probably long gone by the time I left the café."

"I still want to call him and report this." He picked up his cell phone from the coffee table and made the call. When he finished, he hung up and returned his phone to the table. "He'll be out here in a few minutes."

Mary nodded. "I'm sorry, Lucas."

"What on earth are you sorry for?" His gaze held

a gentle warmth. "Mary, sorry about what? I hope you aren't about to tell me that you quit."

"No, nothing like that." She released a deep sigh. "I'm just sorry this note showed up, and now you have to deal with it all."

"Mary, this certainly isn't your fault."

"I just can't imagine who might have left it for me, and why? I want to know if this is a threat I should really take seriously or not."

"Hopefully, Dallas will be able to answer that for you." Lucas held her gaze for a long moment. "I hope you don't have to take it seriously. I would definitely miss you being here."

"You could always hire somebody else." Her heart twisted at the very thought. She loved spending her days with Annabelle and her evenings with Lucas. Even though she hadn't been with them very long, she'd begun to think of them as her family...the family she'd always yearned for but never had.

"I don't want to hire anyone else," he replied firmly, warming her heart despite the slight chill still possessing her body. "You fit with me...uh, and of course, Annabelle absolutely adores you."

Mary smiled and tried to ignore the coldness that still gripped her. "She told me she loved me tonight when I tucked her in," she replied, a nugget of warmth trying to heat through her as she thought of the sweetness of that moment.

"She did?" Lucas looked at her in surprise. "I'm glad she's grown attached to you. She needs a woman's presence in her life, and she doesn't give her heart away lightly."

"She's definitely got my heart," Mary said. "I absolutely love her to death."

Their conversation was interrupted by a knock on the door. Apparently, Dallas had arrived, and all of Mary's muscles and nerves tightened with apprehension. What was Dallas going to say? Would he tell her she needed to leave this place? Was she about to lose this house that had started to feel like her home?

Lucas opened the door to Dallas, who looked more tired than Lucas had ever seen him. "Sorry to bother you," he said to his friend. Lucas knew Dallas had probably been working overtime in an effort to solve Cindy's murder—one of the few murders that had ever occurred in the small town. Not only would Dallas be working the murder case but also any other crime that might take place.

"No problem," Dallas said as Lucas gestured for him to come into the living room. "Hi, Mary," he greeted her as he took a seat on the opposite sofa.

"Hi, Dallas," she returned as Lucas sat in his recliner chair.

"So, what's up?" Dallas asked. He looked at Mary and then at Lucas.

"Mary went to the café for dinner this evening, and when she returned to her car, there was a note on it." Lucas gestured for Mary to hand Dallas the note. As she did, Lucas couldn't help but notice that her hand trembled slightly. Dammit, who had done this? Who was threatening her to get out of his life? Who had frightened her? A protectiveness for her surged up strong inside him.

Dallas read the note, and a muscle ticked in his jaw. "Where was this found?" he asked Mary.

Mary explained how she'd found it under her windshield wiper on her car after eating in the café with Sally Roth. "I just don't know if I really need to be afraid or not," she finally said.

Dallas frowned and read the note once again, then looked at both Mary and Lucas. "It's pretty over the top. It kind of reads like a scorned high school girl. So the question is, who might be jealous that you're here? Lucas, do you know anyone who might not like this arrangement you have with Mary?"

Two names instantly popped into his brain. "Well, Celeste Winthrop has been bringing me home-baked cookies and other goodies on a fairly regular basis." He felt the warmth that suffused his face.

"Now, that's real interesting. Celeste has been showing up at my place occasionally with cookies or brownies," Dallas replied. He shook his head with a wry grin. "I guess she's just doubling down on her efforts to find a new husband for herself."

"So maybe she's not so upset about Mary being here since she still has you to focus on," Lucas said.

"Can you think of anyone else?" Dallas asked.

Lucas changed positions on the sofa. "Gina Hightower… Has she been bringing you meals?"

Dallas shook his head. "No, but I'm assuming she's been bringing you meals?"

"She has. She's made it pretty clear that she'd like to have a romantic relationship with me. So far, I've avoided it by playing dumb. But now that I think about it, when I told her Mary was living here, I don't think she liked it very much. But—honest to God, Dallas—I can't imagine either of those women being so low as to write that nasty note to Mary."

"What do you think, Mary?" Dallas turned his attention to her.

She was curled up in the corner of the sofa, looking small and vulnerable, and once again, a bit of anger for whoever had scared her like this surged inside him. How dare somebody meddle in his life in this way?

"I'm fairly certain both of those women didn't particularly like the fact that I was living here with Lucas, but I can't imagine either one of them stooping so low to get rid of me," she said.

"Then who in your life might not be happy that you're living here?" Dallas asked.

"I…uh…really don't have anyone in my life to object to what I do," she replied softly.

"Nobody?" Dallas looked at her intently. "Nobody you've dated in the past? Maybe somebody who has shown an interest in you recently?"

Her face paled. "I guess there might be somebody who would not be happy with me living here with

Lucas—but he lives in St. Louis, and I can't imagine how he would even know I was here."

"Who is this person?" Dallas asked.

Her cheeks suddenly flamed with color. "His name is Kenny Majors. I…uh…met him on a dating site, although I've never met him in person. I thought he was a really nice man, and things went fairly well for about a month. But then I started noticing some troubling things about him."

"What kind of troubling things?" Dallas asked.

"He had a temper, and he also had a mean streak of jealousy. It finally came to the point where I told him that it wasn't going to work between us, and that's when he exploded. Since that time, he's been sending me very nasty text messages and emails."

The whole time she'd been talking, she stared down at her hands in her lap as if ashamed. Lucas wanted to comfort her, to tell her there was nothing to be ashamed of or embarrassed about. He just didn't understand why she'd decided to involve herself with a dating site when she was so pretty—so charming that there had to be men standing in line right here in town to date her.

She finally looked up at Dallas. "But I don't know why he would come here and leave a note on my car without making any personal contact with me. That just doesn't make sense."

"I'm going to have to see the messages he's been sending to you," Dallas said.

She nodded. "I'll need to get my laptop." She got up from the sofa and left the room.

"Do you really think this guy she's talking about left that note for her?" Lucas asked.

"I don't know what to think right now," Dallas admitted. "Right now, I'm leaning toward a jealous female—but at this point, I want to look at every angle."

"Any breaks in Cindy's murder case?"

Dallas frowned and shook his head. "Unfortunately, that's stalled out. Nobody in town can give me a single reason why anyone would want to hurt Cindy. It's killing me not to find the guilty party. I've never wanted somebody behind bars as much as the person who killed her."

Both men looked at Mary as she returned to the room, her laptop in her arms and a faint blush still coloring her cheeks. They all shifted positions so that Dallas could sit right next to Mary on the sofa and see her computer screen.

"These are all new messages from him," she said softly. "But I'm sure they're in the same vein as the others he's sent."

For the next few minutes, Dallas read Mary's emails and texts. "Whew," he said and finally leaned back against the sofa cushions. "That's some nasty, creepy guy."

Another blush swept into Mary's cheeks. "I wish somebody would have warned me about him before I answered his first message to me."

"Did you turn in his abusive behavior to the dating site?" Dallas asked.

"No… I wasn't sure how to do that, and I was too…too embarrassed," she admitted.

"I'll help you do that tomorrow," Lucas offered, and she flashed him a grateful smile.

She turned back to Dallas. "Do you really think he might have left that note?" Her face suddenly paled again. "Oh, God…do you think he might have killed Cindy and left her body here to warn me about being here in Lucas's home?"

"Whoa, Mary…let's not get ahead of ourselves here. There's no evidence that Cindy's death is in any way tied to the note that was left for you on your car," Dallas said quickly. "In any case, I want you to tell me everything you know about this Kenny Majors creep."

Lucas listened absently as she continued to speak to Dallas. What Lucas was focused on was the tremble of her hands and the way her gaze refused to meet his. He wished he could crawl into her head and see exactly what she was thinking at the moment.

Dallas finally stood up from the sofa. "My gut tells me this note is nothing to worry about—that it's just a nasty piece of work meant to scare you. But I'll check some things out and get back to you."

"Thank you, Dallas," Mary said.

Lucas got up from his chair and smiled at Mary. "I'm going to walk Dallas out. I'll be right back."

The two men walked out into the darkness of the

night. The storm Lucas had noticed moving in earlier was now on top of them. Lightning slashed the sky, followed immediately by a clap of thunder.

"I'll check out this Kenny and see if he's responsible for the note," Dallas said. "But I've got to say, I still suspect it was written by a woman. I guess these things happen when you're the hottest bachelor in town," he added teasingly.

"Stop it," Lucas replied. "You'll let us know what you find out?"

"Definitely." The first raindrops began to fall. "Now, get back inside before you get wet."

Lucas returned to the front porch, where he waited until Dallas had pulled out of the driveway before returning to the living room.

Mary was still on the sofa, still looking a bit embarrassed. "Are you okay?" he asked her.

"I guess," she replied. Her fingers twisted together in her lap.

"Mary, I really don't think you have anything to worry about as far as the note," he said in an attempt to assure her. "And tomorrow, I'll help you make an abuse report concerning this Kenny guy. We can also block him from sending you emails and texts."

Color flashed in her cheeks again. "I'm sorry you had to hear about that. I'm so embarrassed by it all."

"Why would you be embarrassed? You did nothing wrong, Mary. The only thing I wonder is why you were on a dating site in the first place. I would think a woman like you would have plenty of dates from the single men in this town."

She offered him a small smile. "I've had a few dates, but I never connected in any way with the men. I'm not exactly a raving beauty. To be honest, I think I'm fairly invisible working as a checker at the grocery store."

He started to protest but then realized he couldn't invalidate the way she felt. "Well, I will say this—if the single men in this town aren't asking you out on dates, then they're all fools."

Once again, she graced him with a smile. "You're a very nice man, Lucas Maddox. And on that note, I'm ready to call it a night."

She got up from the sofa and grabbed her laptop. Lucas got up as well. He followed her down the hallway to the bedrooms. When she reached her door, she turned around to him.

"Good night, Lucas," she murmured.

Her voice was just above a whisper. Her hair was so shiny and soft looking, and the scent of her permeated the air around him. He suddenly wanted to kiss her. He wanted to feel the spill of her long thick hair in his hands. He felt like he was in a haze, and without thinking of anything else, he took a step toward her.

She didn't step back from him, and then his lips were on hers and his hands were tangled in her hair. For a moment, he was lost in her...in the warmth of her lips, in the silky strands of her hair and in the very scent of her. Instantly, he was aroused as she opened her mouth to him and their tongues swirled together.

A boom of thunder overhead shook the house, and Annabelle cried out, suddenly bringing him back to his senses. He stumbled back from Mary and stared at her. "I…I'm so sorry. That shouldn't have happened."

She nodded and stepped into her room as another crash of thunder sounded and Annabelle cried for him once again. "Go…" she said. "Your daughter needs you." She took another step backward and then closed her bedroom door.

Chapter 6

He'd kissed her. It had been beyond wonderful. His lips had been masterful as they plied hers with a heat that immediately stoked a fire deep inside her. The kiss had shocked and surprised her, and she was still thinking about it long after she got into bed.

For about an hour, rain pattered against the window and was punctuated by thunder and lightning. The storm outside reflected the chaos of her thoughts.

Why had he kissed her? Was it simply because he wanted to, or had it been out of pity? The conversation before had revealed her to be a woman nobody dated, a woman who couldn't even get internet dating right. How embarrassing. How utterly pathetic. Was that what had prompted the kiss? Pity?

The night had been filled with such high emotion. She'd enjoyed having dinner with Sally but then received the troubling note. She'd been feeling worried about the note when Annabelle said she loved her. She'd then found herself having to confess just how bad she was at choosing men. And then…the kiss.

She finally fell asleep but awoke the next morning with more than a little anxiety over seeing Lucas again. Would he want to talk about the kiss, or would he pretend it had never happened?

She certainly didn't intend to say anything about it. She was hoping it would be business as usual between them. With this thought in mind, she got out of bed, showered and dressed for the day.

As she left her room, the scent of coffee permeated the air, letting her know Lucas was already up and probably in the kitchen. It was still too early for Annabelle to be awake. Her heart still warmed with the little girl's words of love the night before.

When she entered the kitchen, Lucas was seated at the table with a cup of coffee and the newspaper before him. He looked up as she entered and smiled at her. "Good morning."

"Good morning to you. That coffee smells good." She headed to the cabinet to get herself a cup. After getting the drink, she sat opposite him at the table.

"How did you sleep?" he asked.

"It took me a little while to wind down, but once I did, I slept fine," she replied.

"Good." His smile fell, and he frowned. "Mary,

about last night… I apologize for crossing the lines of professionalism. I hope you'll forgive me and know that it will never happen again. It was just a crazy night, and I was way out of line."

"It's okay. There's nothing to forgive," she replied, embarrassed to even talk about it.

"I just need you to know that I would never want to put you in an uncomfortable position," he continued.

"Really, it's okay, Lucas."

He held her gaze for a long moment. "So it's business as usual?"

"Absolutely." She smiled at him, hoping it would put an end to this conversation.

"Do you have anything exciting planned for today before you get back to work tomorrow?" he asked.

"No, I'm just planning on relaxing and playing with Annabelle," she replied.

"I need to go into town later to order some supplies. Do you want to come with us?" he asked.

"I'd love to. There are a few things I could pick up from the grocery store, if that would be okay."

"Sure. Why don't we plan to leave here about ten thirty, and we can shop and then eat lunch at the café?"

"That sounds good," she agreed. It would be nice to get out of the house before her workweek started the next day. Maybe the fresh air and sunshine would take away the memory of his wonderful kiss, but she seriously doubted it.

"And now I'm going to get some breakfast going." He got up from the table and went over to the refrigerator, where he withdrew a package of bacon.

"You want some help?" she asked, feeling guilty for just sitting there, even though it was her day off.

"No, I'm good. I'm just going to fry up some bacon, and then I'll make some scrambled eggs once Annabelle gets up."

While he got the bacon frying, they talked about Annabelle. "How long did it take you to get her back to sleep last night?" Mary asked.

"Thankfully, not long. I sat next to her bed and told her stories about the thunder gods until she fell asleep again."

Mary smiled at him. "Thunder-god stories? I wonder if those are as good as my sleep-fairy stories."

Lucas laughed. "I guess they both serve the same purpose when it comes to putting her to sleep."

"I've told you before, you're lucky she goes to bed as well as she does. She doesn't even mind nap time. She never gives me any problems."

Lucas turned over the sizzling bacon. "Yeah, she's always been easy in that way. And once she falls asleep, she almost never gets up in the middle of the night...unless there is thunder."

"It must have been really hard on you, losing your wife when Annabelle was just a baby."

He turned from the stove to look at her. "To be honest, having Annabelle probably saved my life. She was my sole reason to get out of bed each morning, to put one foot in front of the other and keep going. Without her, I'm not sure where my grief would have taken me."

At that moment, the subject of their discussion ran into the kitchen, all giggles and smiles. "Good morning, bug," Lucas said.

"Daddy, I not a bug," she replied with another burst of giggles. "I a girl." She turned to Mary. "Up?" she asked, wanting to get into her booster seat.

"What else do you say?" Mary asked.

"Up, peeze?"

"Good girl," Mary replied and then stood up to help her into the booster seat.

"Are you ready to eat some scrambled eggs?" Lucas asked as he took the last of the crispy bacon out of the skillet.

"Scrambled eggs, yes," Annabelle replied and clapped her hands together.

"I'll get out some plates and silverware," Mary said.

It was just after eight when they were seated at the table and eating breakfast. "Daddy has to go to the feed store today and order some farming stuff," he told his daughter.

"And I get a present?" Annabelle asked.

"You still have to earn three more stars before you get a present," Mary said before Lucas could reply.

"Then no present today," Annabelle said with a sad face.

"Not today," Lucas replied. "Maybe next time you'll have your ten stars and can get your present."

Mary smiled at him. It felt good to be on the same page. It also felt good to teach Annabelle that presents just didn't come automatically—they had to be earned.

They finished breakfast, and Mary helped with the cleanup, then returned to her room to get ready for the trip into town. Once again, she found herself thinking about that kiss.

She knew it was best for them not to mix business with pleasure, that developing any kind of a personal relationship with him could put everything in jeopardy. Even knowing all that, she wouldn't protest if he decided to kiss her again. In fact, she secretly hoped he *would* kiss her again.

They left the house at ten o'clock. Mary had decided to wear a pair of black capris with a black-and-pink sleeveless summer blouse. Annabelle had insisted she wear a pair of black shorts with a pink blouse like Mary's. She also wanted her hair pulled into a ponytail just like Mary was wearing.

It was a form of flattery that touched her heart. Mary also didn't take lightly the responsibility in knowing she was becoming a person Annabelle wanted to emulate.

"I hope some of that rain last night helped all the crops," Mary said as they passed the various fields on the way into town. Despite the rain the night before, today was as hot and humid as ever.

"It didn't hurt," Lucas replied. "In fact, I wish it would have rained a couple more hours than it did. It's been so dry this year that most of us have been having to water the fields more than usual."

"That's too bad."

"That's farming," he said. "We're always at the whims of the weather. It will take me about twenty minutes or so in the feed shop. After that, we'll go have lunch and then stop at the grocery store for whatever we need before going home. Does that sound okay with you?"

"Sounds perfect to me," she replied. "Annabelle and I will just sit in the truck and wait for you while you're in the feed store." She looked back to where Annabelle was strapped into her car seat. "We can wait in the truck for Daddy. Right, Annabelle?"

"Right," she replied and kicked her feet enthusiastically.

Minutes later, Lucas was in the feed store. "What do you want to eat for lunch?" she asked Annabelle.

"Grilled cheese and mashed 'tatoes and mac and cheese and ice cream," Annabelle said.

Mary laughed. "You sound like a hungry little girl."

"I a hungry girl," Annabelle agreed.

A butterfly flew by the window. "A sutterby," Annabelle said with a squeal. "Look, Ms. Mary, it's a sutterby."

"Yes, it's a butterfly," Mary said.

"I love it," Annabelle replied.

The conversation turned to all things butterfly. They talked about red ones and spotted ones and bright yellow ones. They had moved on to talking about Annabelle's baby dolls by the time Lucas returned to the truck.

"All set to go to the café for lunch?" he asked, looking at his daughter in the rearview mirror.

"Daddy, I ready. I a hungry little girl," she said.

"And I'm a hungry big girl," Mary added with a laugh.

"Well, then, I'd better feed the girls in my life right now," he said.

The girls in his life. His words warmed a place deep in Mary's heart. It was a warmth she knew she shouldn't embrace, but she couldn't help the way it made her feel.

She repeated to him what Annabelle had said she wanted for lunch. He laughed. "I think we might be editing that down a bit once we actually order."

On a Sunday afternoon, the café was packed. It was the only day of the week that a hostess was there to seat people. When they walked in, they were told it would be just a minute for them to be seated at a booth with a booster seat.

True to the hostess's word, they were almost immediately accommodated. Mary suspected it was because nobody wanted a three-year-old getting tired and cranky and throwing a fit while waiting for a table.

As they were led to the booth, they passed a table

with Celeste Winthrop and a man Mary didn't recognize. Mary could have sworn Celeste narrowed her eyes and stared at her balefully. Thankfully, once they were seated in the booth, Mary couldn't see Celeste. Still, she couldn't help but wonder if she had been the one who had left the note under her windshield wiper.

They managed to convince Annabelle that what she wanted for lunch was a grilled-cheese sandwich and fries, with the promise of ice cream for dessert.

Lucas ordered a bacon cheeseburger and Mary opted for a chef salad. Once their drinks were served, they started talking about the forecast of more hot weather for the coming week and what work he intended to accomplish in the fields.

He'd been talking for several minutes when he grimaced and shook his head. "I apologize. I'm probably boring you silly with all this farm talk."

"'Farm talk,'" Annabelle echoed.

"That's right," Lucas said to his daughter with a smile.

"No, you are not boring me at all," Mary replied truthfully. "I can't believe I grew up here and never thought much about the farmers and the different kinds of crops in the area."

He grinned at her. "That's because you were a town kid, and us country kids didn't hang out with the town kids. We had to get right home after school to work on our family farms. I was working in the fields when I was ten years old." He paused a moment and then continued. "I also had to walk ten miles uphill to school every day in blizzard conditions, and back home uphill in the sweltering heat."

She laughed. "Poor baby." She sobered somewhat. "But it was true about you being ten and working, right?"

He nodded. "That's true."

"Did you resent it at all?" she asked curiously.

"Not a bit. I was proud to know I was helping my father. I loved working alongside him." There was a faint whisper of longing in his voice.

"You miss him," she observed.

"Yeah, I do. But I'm glad he's happy and doing what he wants to do. He worked hard for years to make the farm a real success for me, so he's earned whatever life he wants to live now."

Their conversation halted when their food arrived. "I was thinking maybe one night this week, it might be fun to plan a little picnic on the back patio," Mary said, watching his expression to see if he'd think the idea was stupid.

"I think that sounds like fun," he immediately replied. "It will be Annabelle's very first picnic." Annabelle smiled at the mention of her name and then popped a fry into her mouth.

"Then why don't I plan for it on Wednesday night?" she said.

"Sounds perfect to me." He smiled at her. "I'm glad we have you in our lives, Mary."

Her cheeks warmed. "I'm glad to be in your lives," she replied.

"I glad, too," Annabelle said with a big grin. Mary and Lucas both laughed.

"Tell me more about the crops you grow," Mary said.

"Are you really sure you want to hear about that?"

"I'm sure—otherwise I wouldn't have asked," she replied. "I want to know about the things you do when you're out in the fields."

It was true; she wanted to understand what he did and how the farm ran. She wanted to know everything about him. She wished she could crawl into his head and know all his thoughts. Did he have dreams for himself, or had the death of his wife stolen those dreams away?

"Well, don't you all look happy?" Nicole Dennis appeared at the side of their booth.

"Hi, Nicole. Want to join us?" Lucas asked. Mary immediately scooted over to make room for Nicole to sit next to her.

"No, thanks. I'm having lunch with a couple of my friends," she replied and gestured to another table where two women had just been seated. "I just wanted to come by and say hello." She pointed at Lucas's plate. "Oh, remember how much Diana loved the burgers here? Lucas, I'm sure she's looking down on you right now with all the love she had in her heart."

Mary watched as the light in Lucas's eyes dimmed. "I know, Nicole. I miss her, too," he said.

"Well, enjoy the rest of your meal. I'll stop by the house sometime later this week," Nicole said, and then she joined the other ladies at their table.

The mood shifted after that. Lucas grew quiet and withdrawn. Annabelle seemed to pick up on her father's mood and she, too, ate quietly.

Mary knew Nicole meant well, but by just reminding Lucas of her daughter's never-ending love for him, she'd apparently cast him back into the depths of his grief.

It saddened her that this wonderful, kind man would continue to keep his heart closed off to love in his future. It also made her sad for Annabelle, who would never know the love of a caring stepmother as she grew up.

Mary knew if she continued to work for Lucas, her job would probably end in two years, when Annabelle started school. During that time, all she could do was support Lucas and love Annabelle. And forget the kiss that had momentarily rocked her world.

"I just need to pick up a few things," Mary said as they parked in front of the grocery store.

"That's okay. We'll all go in. I might want to sneak a few things into the basket," Lucas replied.

"Like what?" she asked.

He grinned at her. "Like some ice cream and maybe a cake."

"Ice cream!" Annabelle repeated and clapped her hands together.

The three of them walked inside, and Luke grabbed a shopping cart. "I didn't know you had a sweet tooth," Mary said to him. "I can definitely start making you desserts if you tell me what you like."

As they walked the aisles, he told Mary what kinds of desserts he enjoyed. With each dish he mentioned, Annabelle added her two cents by clapping her hands enthusiastically. Mary's musical laughter added to the fun.

In the bakery department, Lucas found a chocolate cake covered with chocolate icing and colorful sprinkles, and it promptly made its way into the cart. Annabelle approved of his choice; she loved anything with sprinkles.

They turned down an aisle and immediately ran into Gina Hightower. She greeted them all with a bright smile. "Lucas, could I talk to you for a moment... alone?" she surprised him by asking. "Maybe in the next aisle?"

"Oh...okay." He looked at Mary and his daughter. "I'll be right back."

He followed Gina to the next aisle. "What's up?" he asked. As usual, the attractive woman was dressed to the nines in a white sundress and a thick gold necklace and matching earrings.

"Lucas, I've kept my feelings inside for a while now, but I think it's time for you to know I'm positively crazy about you."

He stared at her. Was she really having this conversation with him? Was she really professing her undying love for him in the middle of the canned-vegetable aisle?

"Gina, I'm sorry. I guess I should have told you before now. Maybe you don't know just how deeply I've mourned over Diana. After her death, I decided I have no intention of ever dating or marrying again."

"Oh." Her cheeks flushed pink. "Well, then, this is rather awkward."

"I'm sorry, Gina. If I led you on in any way—"

"You didn't. I was just hoping…" Her voice trailed off and she looked away. Then she looked back at him and smiled. "Don't worry. We can still be friends."

"Of course we can," he agreed. "I appreciate that."

She stepped back from him as a couple came down the aisle. "I'll just see you around town," she said, and then she turned and pushed her cart in the opposite direction.

Lucas stared after her for a long moment. He felt bad. It had taken a lot of courage for her to speak her mind, and then he had shot her down.

"Everything okay?" Mary asked when he returned to her and Annabelle.

"Everything is fine," he assured her. "Let's go see what kind of ice cream we can find."

Everything remained fine for the next several days.

"We need to get the sprinklers to the other field,"

Lucas said to the men who worked for him on Wednesday morning.

"We can drive them over and get them working in an hour or so," Jack Abrams replied.

"The soybeans definitely need the extra water that the spring rain didn't bring," Adam Schwartz agreed.

"Then let's get on that this morning," Lucas said.

Two hours later, the sprinklers had been moved and now slowly worked their way over the field of soybeans. Soybeans and corn were the main crops that made Lucas a comfortable living.

But farming was always a crapshoot. Weather conditions could destroy a crop; so could bugs and wildlife. Thankfully, everything looked nice and healthy this year, and when harvesting time came, he hoped to get a good yield.

It was five o'clock when he made his way to the house. As he walked in through the back door, he was greeted by Mary's bright smile and Annabelle's happy voice.

"Daddy, we having a nikpic," she exclaimed.

Lucas looked at his daughter with confusion; then he remembered. "It's a *picnic*," he replied, grinning at Mary.

"Yeah, a nitpick," Annabelle replied. "We eat outside."

"That's right," Mary said. She looked back at Lucas, her green eyes shining brightly. "I've got everything ready on the back porch whenever you're ready. You and Annabelle can get settled in outside, and then I'll bring the food out."

"Sounds like a plan. All I need to do is wash up. I'll be right back." He left the kitchen and went into his bathroom to clean up.

For the last three years, he'd dreaded walking into the house after a day outside at work. While he'd appreciated Nicole watching Annabelle during the day, the minute he walked in the door, he felt her grief. The house was dark and desolate, even with Annabelle's smiles and rambunctious energy.

Now he looked forward to coming home and being greeted by Mary's smiles and sunny disposition. She appeared genuinely interested in what he'd done and how his day had gone. Annabelle was always in a happy mood when he walked through the door. It was as if Mary's positive attitude rubbed off on her, too.

He finished with his quick shower, then dressed and returned to the kitchen, where Annabelle and Mary were waiting. "Okay, you two…scoot outside, and the rest of the food will be coming very soon."

"Are you ready, Annabelle?" he asked. She nodded enthusiastically. "Then let's go outside to our picnic."

He walked outside and was surprised by all Mary had accomplished in pulling the picnic together. Three of the colorful cushions that had been on his outdoor chairs were now on the patio at the edges of a red-and-black flannel blanket he'd almost forgotten he owned.

She must have found his cooler in the utility room, because it now sat in the center of the blanket. "Sit, Daddy," Annabelle instructed and pointed to one of the cushions.

Once he was seated, Annabelle sat and then clapped her hands. "Now is nitpik time," she said happily.

Mary stepped out of the back door with a plate of fried chicken in her hand. "Oh, wow, that looks delicious," Lucas said, laughing when his stomach rumbled loud enough for the two females to hear.

"Now, that sounds like a hungry tummy," Mary said with a grin. She gracefully sat on the last cushion and then placed the chicken in front of her.

"Annabelle, do you want to get out our plates?" she asked.

Annabelle nodded and crawled over to the cooler. She managed to wrestle off the lid and then withdrew colorful paper plates. "One for Daddy," she said, placing one in front of him. "One for Ms. Mary and one for Annabelle. Did I do it right, Ms. Mary?"

"You did it perfectly," Mary replied. She pulled out silverware and then handed Annabelle a carton of milk. Lucas's favorite beer was icy cold, and Mary had a soda. She then began to pull a variety of containers out of the cooler. "We have potato salad, baked beans and bread-and-butter sandwiches," she said. "There are cubes of cheese and apple slices, and for dessert there's a strawberry cake."

"I iced the cake, Daddy," Annabelle said as Mary helped her fill her plate.

"That's wonderful, Annabelle. You're getting to be such a big girl," he replied.

"I a big girl," she agreed proudly. "I get stars."

"That's terrific," Lucas replied.

As Lucas filled his plate, he couldn't help but notice how pretty Mary looked. She was clad in a pair of cutoff jeans, exposing the lovely length of her shapely legs. Her blouse was a navy blue sleeveless that hugged her slender waist and showcased her medium-sized breasts.

Her hair was tied at the nape of her neck and fell down her back in a low ponytail, sparkling with golden highlights. Lucas couldn't imagine why men weren't beating down her door to date her.

He suspected it had to do with her shyness. When it was just him and Annabelle, Mary wasn't shy; but he'd noticed that when they were in town or around other people, she seemed to climb into a shell.

Her shyness wasn't on display at the moment as they ate and laughed at Annabelle's silly antics. Mary even taught them a funny little song about picnics and ants. As they tried to sing it, they dissolved into laughter more than once.

It felt good. It felt so damned good. It seemed as if his laughter had been stolen away from him for far too long, and it felt wonderful to find it again.

The food was excellent, and the picnic was a rousing success. When they were finished eating, Mary and Lucas remained seated on the cushions and watched Annabelle play in the backyard.

She brought out two of her baby dolls and disappeared into her playhouse, where every couple of minutes, she appeared at the window to tell them something.

"This has been really nice," he said to Mary. "Thank you for setting this up."

"I just thought it might be fun for Annabelle to experience a *nitpik*," she replied.

He laughed again. "She was thrilled by the idea of eating outside."

"Yes, she was," Mary agreed.

"Hi, Daddy. Hi, Ms. Mary," Annabelle yelled out the playhouse window. "Baby Sue is sleeping, and baby Annie is being bad."

"Put her in time-out," Mary shouted back.

"'Kay." Annabelle disappeared from the window again.

"You haven't mentioned having to put her in time-out lately," he said.

"She's been good lately. She really wants to please you and me, and I've learned some of the things that might trigger a temper tantrum. I've been attempting to head them off before they happen."

"You're very good with her. Do you want to have your own children?"

A wistful glow filled her pretty green eyes. "In a perfect world—if I was in a happy, loving marriage—then I would want to have my own children."

"How many would you want?" he asked curiously.

"Two at the very least. Growing up as an only

child, I always felt like I missed out in not having a sibling. I was terribly lonely as a child, but I think that had to do more with my distant parents than anything else."

He gazed toward the playhouse, his thoughts on his own daughter. Would she be lonely without any siblings? Would she turn out to be well-adjusted? He looked back at Mary. "But you turned out all right."

She laughed. "I think I turned out okay." Her gaze softened, and she smiled at him. "Lucas, the difference between Annabelle and me is she has an engaged, loving father who she can depend on being there for her at any time."

"Yeah, but is that enough?" he asked.

"You are enough," she assured him. "As long as you remain loving and open to having dialogues with her throughout her growing-up years, you will be more than enough for her."

"Thanks, Mary." Once again, he was surprised by a sudden swift desire for her. It wasn't just the fact that he found her physically attractive—he was drawn to her innate softness and the way she loved his daughter. He liked the way she assured him when he was feeling doubtful about the way *he* loved his daughter.

He wanted to lean across the blanket and capture her soft lips with his. He wanted to scoop her up in his arms and carry her to his bed. He wanted to lose himself in her warmth, in her lilac scent and in the softness of her eyes.

"Daddy, look at me." Annabelle's voice sliced through the haze of desire that had momentarily gripped him.

Lucas got to his feet. He needed to gain some distance from Mary before he did something stupid. "Come on, Annabelle. It's time to go inside now."

"Five more minutes, 'kay?" she replied. "Five more minutes, peeze?"

"Okay, five more minutes, and then it's time to go inside and get into a bath," he replied.

He bent down and grabbed the dirty paper plates to toss in the trash. "I'll take care of the rest," Mary said as she also got to her feet.

"I can help," he replied. He tossed the cushions back to the chairs where they belonged as she put the containers back into the cooler.

Once everything was packed up, he grabbed the cooler, and she picked up the blanket and refolded it. "Come on, Annabelle. It's time to go inside now," he said. He consciously kept his gaze off Mary, still fighting the desire that wanted to sweep through him.

What was wrong with him? He was grateful that Mary had brought back some joy into his life. But this desire, which not only felt like want but also felt like an irrational need, would complicate his life in ways he couldn't even imagine if he gave in to it.

Still, if he did give in to it, how would Mary react?

Would she welcome his advances, or would she soundly reject him?

And, dammit, why was he even speculating on it?

Chapter 7

Saturday night, Mary checked her reflection in the mirror. Tonight, she was meeting Sally and Marianne Smith, another grocery store clerk, at Murphy's, a popular bar in town. She knew Lucas had asked Nicole to babysit, and his plan was to go to the Farmer's Club for a couple of hours.

There had been a strange tension in the air since the evening of the picnic. Nothing had changed in their evening routine, and yet she'd noticed at times that something was different in the way Lucas looked at her.

It was something that made her breath hitch in the back of her throat, that sent a shocking wave of heat through her veins. The hard glint in his eyes looked like desire. Even thinking about it now shot a shiver of deliciousness up her spine.

If desire was what he was feeling, she was relatively sure that it wasn't for her specifically but probably grown in the intimacy and domestic aspects of their daily life.

They were effectively living as husband and wife, except for the fact that they went to different bedrooms at bedtime. Maybe it was some sort of transference on his part from his dead wife to her and she shouldn't really be surprised.

What she did wonder was, if he made an advance on her, what would she do? She found him to be incredibly sexy, and there was a part of her that would love to throw caution to the wind and make love with him.

However, could she do that knowing he didn't really love her? Could she do that knowing it might mess up the harmony they'd achieved in their daily life? That it might jeopardize her job and her home?

She shoved all these thoughts out of her head and turned away from the mirror. Murphy's called for casual clothing, so she was wearing jeans and a red fitted, sleeveless blouse.

She was looking forward to the evening out. Hanging out with Sally and Marianne was always a good time, and it wouldn't hurt to get some distance from Lucas and the wild energy that had snapped in the air between them lately.

At seven, she left her bedroom and walked out

into the living room, where Nicole was seated on the sofa with a child's book in her hand. Annabelle was sitting next to her.

"Hi, Nicole," Mary said.

"Hello, Mary. Lucas told me you're going to Murphy's this evening."

"Yes, I'm meeting a couple of friends from the grocery store there," Mary replied.

"That sounds like fun."

Mary smiled at the older woman. "It should be fun. And, Annabelle, you need to let Granny tuck you into bed tonight."

"No Ms. Mary?"

"No Ms. Mary tonight," Mary said firmly.

"You get Granny tonight," Nicole said to the little girl. "Isn't that nice?"

Annabelle nodded. "Ms. Mary, Granny is reading me a story."

"That's nice. Are you being a good listener?" Mary asked.

Annabelle nodded once again. "I a good girl. I listen."

"You are a really good girl," Nicole said and hugged Annabelle.

"I shouldn't be too late tonight," Mary said. "I'll probably be back around ten thirty or eleven at the latest. I'm not really much of a night person."

At that moment, Lucas came into the living room. He looked as hot as she'd ever seen him, in jeans and a royal blue polo shirt that matched his beautiful eyes. She wished she was going dancing with Lucas. She wished she was going anywhere with him.

His gaze was warm on her. "Mary, you look nice," he said.

"You clean up pretty well yourself," she replied with a smile. "And now it's time for me to get out of here. Good night, Nicole. Good night, Lucas."

A few minutes later, she was in her car, driving into town. She tried not to think about Lucas and the little girl who had captured her heart and instead focused on the night ahead.

Murphy's was kind of a dive bar, but it was popular with the single set in town. The Farmer's Club catered to a more mature crowd. Where Murphy's music was cranked up loud, she'd heard the music at the Farmer's Club was more subdued and that there was also no dance floor.

She'd been to Murphy's dozens of times, but she'd never been in the Farmer's Club. She hoped Lucas enjoyed himself there this evening. He worked so hard during the week; he deserved to toss back a few beers with friends.

Murphy's was located on the outskirts of town. It was a low, flat building with neon beer signs popping at every window. Mary pulled up to an empty space in the third row of the parking lot, right next to Sally's car.

"Hey, girl," Sally greeted her when they were both out of their vehicles. "I don't think Marianne is here yet. Should we hang around out here and see if she arrives in the next few minutes?"

"Sure, we can wait out here," Mary agreed. Even though it was warm, it was a pleasant evening without a cloud in the sky.

The two visited until Marianne pulled in beside them. Marianne was married and the relatively new mother of a three-month-old little boy.

"Sorry I'm late," she said as she approached them after parking her car. She pulled her curly red hair up into a messy ponytail on top of her head. "I barely got out of the house alive. I promised David I would change Noah's diaper right before I left. When I did, my beautiful, precious little boy peed all over me, prompting me to have to change my clothes."

"Ah, the joys of little boys," Mary said with a laugh.

"Well, I'm eager to get inside and see if I can find the joy of a *grown-up* boy," Sally replied, making Marianne and Mary laugh.

"What about you, Mary? Are you as hungry for a man as Sally?"

"If a good one comes around, I wouldn't kick him to the curb. But my time is pretty full right now with my job."

"And you're going to tell me all about your job when we get inside," Marianne said.

They managed to get a table toward the back, where the music wasn't quite so loud and they could easily carry on a conversation. Sally was the only one to order an alcoholic drink; Mary and Marianne ordered sodas.

Almost immediately, Sally hit the dance floor with a guy named Craig, who Mary knew worked as an auto mechanic at the garage.

"We miss you at the grocery store," Marianne said. "You were the only person there that always kept a sunny smile on your face and a good attitude in your heart."

"Thanks, Marianne. I miss seeing you and Sally every day, but I love working for Lucas. I've totally fallen in love with his daughter."

"What about the man himself? Sally told me you have a crush on him."

Mary laughed. "Sally talks too much—but I'll confess, I do have a little crush on him."

"Heck, *I* have a little crush on him just from checking him out at the grocery store. Who wouldn't have a crush on that hot, hunky man?" Marianne fanned her face with her hand, making Mary laugh again.

"So, how is that little boy of yours?"

Marianne sobered. "I've never loved anyone as much as I love Noah. Mary, it's a kind of love I've never experienced before. You need to find a good man, get married and have a baby. Only then will you understand what I'm talking about," Marianne said.

"Right now, I'm not really looking for a man. Maybe once this job ends and I have my teaching degree, then I'll be ready for romance." That had always been Mary's plan.

It had been in a moment of loneliness that she'd joined that stupid dating site and met Kenny. Luckily, the day after her talk with Dallas, Lucas had helped her report Kenny to the site, and he'd also shown her how to block his texts and emails. So over the last couple of days, the abusive communication from him had stopped.

Sally came back to the table, and the conversation turned to town gossip. With Sally's flair for the dramatic, she had both Mary and Marianne rolling with laughter as she repeated the most outlandish gossip she'd heard in the last week.

Mary was asked to dance twice. Jeff Wyland was a nice guy who worked in the post office, and Ethan Dourty worked in the one insurance agency in town. They were both good men, but there was no spark there. She'd danced with both of them before when she'd been here.

Several times during the evening, she wondered about Lucas. Was he enjoying his night out? Was he talking to other farmers in the area? Had he given her a single thought while he was out?

She mentally kicked herself. Why on earth would he think about her? She was just the nanny and housekeeper. Still, she couldn't help but think about the energy that had crackled in the air between them for the past several days. She definitely hadn't been able to stop thinking about the kiss they had shared.

It was just after nine when Marianne called it a night. "I need to get back home and rescue my husband. Noah is usually fussy and hard to get to sleep at night."

The three hugged, and then Marianne left. "You aren't going to poop out on me so early, are you?" Sally asked Mary.

"I'll stay for a little while longer," Mary replied, even though she was more than ready to head back.

She'd always enjoyed coming out with Sally to Murphy's, but tonight she realized she'd rather be home with Annabelle or watching television with Lucas. *Funny how priorities can change*, she thought.

She stayed until just after ten, and then she told Sally she was ready to call it a night. Sally decided to stay, so she and Sally said their goodbyes, and then Mary left the bar.

Once she was in her car, a wave of tiredness swept over her. She stifled a yawn, mentally laughing at herself. What an old lady she'd become...ready for bed at ten o'clock on a Saturday night.

She drove through town to get on the road that would take her to Lucas's home. At this time of night, Millsville looked like a ghost town, with all the stores closed up and nobody on the streets.

When the town was in her rearview mirror, she hit the long stretch of dark road that would take her to the farm. There was nobody else on the narrow two-lane highway, which was flanked with deep ditches and trees on either side.

She turned up her radio to fill the silence as she drove. She was about halfway between town and Lucas's place when she saw headlights behind her. She was going the speed limit, but the other vehicle was coming up on her fast.

She could now see that it was some kind of van or a pickup truck. It also appeared to be drifting back and forth across the center line. *The driver must be drunk*, she thought as she watched the vehicle go from lane to lane.

She moved over as far as she could so the truck could easily go around her. She gasped as the truck banged into the back of her car, causing the steering wheel to jump out of her hands.

What had happened? The person had to be drunk. But it didn't matter—they slammed into the back of her car once again. Mary cried out as she tried to maintain control of her vehicle.

She stepped on the gas in an attempt to gain some distance. Why was this happening? Who was driving that truck? Was the bumping some sort of a mistake… an accident? Or was it an attack?

Her breaths came out in panicked gasps. She had no time to think about the *who* or the *why*; the truck sped up and clipped the corner of her bumper, sending her into a spin. She tried to correct but couldn't as the car careened out of control.

The seat belt snapped painfully tight against her chest, expelling what little air was in her lungs. She became disoriented as the car continued to spin. She had a single moment to know she was in deep trouble.

Finally, she screamed as her car left the road and went airborne.

Lucas leaned back on his bar stool and took a sip of his second beer of the night. It had been a relaxing evening. He'd spent most of his time talking to Amos Winters, an old-timer who had been farming in the area for over fifty years.

Amos was a colorful character. He'd been married five times and had twelve children and dozens of grandchildren. He was a font of information about farming and crops—some good and some pure baloney. Still, Lucas always learned something when talking to the old man, and he was always entertained by him. Amos had just left, and so for the moment, Lucas found himself sitting alone at the long, polished bar.

There wasn't a big crowd here tonight. Several people were playing shuffleboard in the back, while others sat in booths, eating bar food.

"You sure I can't get you anything, Lucas?" Ranger Simmons, the owner of the place, asked him. Ranger was an old-timer who had given his farm to his son. He had opened the Farmer's Club almost twenty years ago and now lived in a room above the place. He was a nice man whom everyone in town liked and admired.

"Nah, I'm good, Ranger."

"From what I hear, you're doing *very* good with

that pretty little grocery store clerk working for you," Ranger said with a sly grin and a wink.

Lucas laughed. "It's not like that, Ranger. She and I have a wonderful working relationship, but that's all."

"I figured as much, but you know how gossip flies around this town. Anyway, let me know if I can get you anything from the kitchen." With that, Ranger grabbed a wet towel and began wiping down the bar.

What was Mary doing right now? She'd looked so pretty when she'd left the house. For the past week, he'd been acutely aware of her. The desire he felt for her that had struck him at odd times of the day or evening now thrummed inside his veins all the time.

He tried to think about Diana and the love he felt for her. He tried to remember that he had vowed to love his wife forever...through eternity.

However, she'd been gone for over three long years. Diana didn't fill his evenings with conversation and laughter. Kissing her photo didn't warm his lips or make his heart beat faster.

Would he feel this same kind of desire for any other woman who was cooking his evening meals and taking care of his daughter? No...it was all Mary.

He loved how she greeted him after a hard day in the fields. He also loved the sound of her laughter, and he found himself working to be clever and funny just so he'd hear those musical notes.

He'd seen the way she'd get down on the floor and

play with Annabelle, how easily she slipped into make-believe. It was obvious Annabelle loved Ms. Mary.

If he was going to feel desire for anyone, then why not for Celeste or Gina? Both were attractive women and had indicated to him that they'd be up for anything he wanted.

However, neither of them stirred his blood the way Mary did. Neither of them made sweet, hot desire flood through his veins. It was all Mary. There was no doubt she had awakened a part of him that he'd thought he'd buried with Diana.

And he didn't know what to do about it. He knew what he *should* do: he should leave it alone. He should leave *her* alone and not pursue anything outside of their professional working relationship. And that was what he intended to do—but he also knew it was going to be a hell of a challenge for him.

His phone vibrated in his pocket. He pulled it out to see Dallas's number on the caller ID. He answered, wondering why the lawman would be calling him on a Saturday night. "Dallas, what's up?"

"Lucas, there's been an accident." Dallas's words instantly tightened all of Lucas's muscles. He immediately thought of Nicole and Annabelle.

"What kind of an accident?" he asked tersely as his heart began to race.

"It's Mary. She's been in a car accident."

"How bad?" Lucas got up from his stool and threw a handful of bills on the bar, his heart now banging against his rib cage.

"Her car rolled a couple of times."

"Where is she now?" Lucas headed for the exit.

"She's in an ambulance and headed to the hospital."

Lucas didn't wait to hear any more. All he knew was he had to get to the hospital as soon as possible. He left the bar and then raced for his truck in the parking lot.

Once he was heading down the road toward the hospital, questions flew through his mind. Her car had rolled a couple of times? What on earth had happened? Had she had too much to drink? He found it hard to believe that she would risk her life or somebody else's by having too much to drink and then getting behind the wheel of a car.

Right now, it didn't matter what had caused the wreck. Her car had rolled? Oh, God, he should have asked Dallas about her condition. Was she badly hurt?

His hands tightened on the steering wheel as he thought of her broken and bleeding. Was she barely clinging to life right now? Not Mary. He couldn't stand the idea of her hurting. He couldn't stand the idea of her...

He checked that horrendous thought before it could complete itself and stepped on the gas. Thankfully, the hospital wasn't too far away from the Farmer's Club.

He sped down the road, and when he reached the small hospital, he wheeled into the parking lot. He stopped his truck in a parking space and jumped out. His heart was still pounding in an accelerated rhythm that made him feel half-sick to his stomach.

When he reached the emergency waiting room, Gloria Young was behind the desk. She was a pretty young woman with short blond hair. There was nobody else in the waiting room.

"Gloria, Mary Curtis was brought in by ambulance. Can you tell somebody I need an update about her condition as soon as possible?"

"Will do." She immediately got up and disappeared through a door that said Authorized Personnel Only.

Lucas paced the floor, fear for Mary aching in his tightening chest. Gloria came back out. "Dr. Erickson will be out to speak to you when he can," she said and returned to her seat.

When he can? What did that mean? Was Mary going to have to have some sort of surgery? At least he knew that Alexander Erickson was a good doctor and surgeon.

Alex had been two years older than Lucas in school, and he'd always known he wanted to be a doctor. Millsville was lucky he'd decided to practice here in his small hometown instead of heading for far greener pastures in a big city. He worked at the hospital, and he also had his own practice.

Lucas continued to pace as the minutes ticked by. After an hour had passed, he sat in one of the uncomfortable green plastic chairs. He dropped his head into his hands as worry continued to eat at him.

What was happening? When would the doctor be out to tell him her condition? Should he call Mary's parents? The idea flitted through his head, but he immediately dismissed it. Mary had made it clear that she had no relationship with them. In any case, it really wasn't his place to contact them.

He suddenly realized that, other than her friends, he was all she had. A glance at his phone let him know it was almost midnight. He made a quick phone call to Nicole to let her know what was happening and that he was going to be late.

She assured him that was fine; she'd been napping on the sofa and Annabelle was asleep. She told him she hoped Mary was okay and that she'd just see him when he got home. At least Lucas knew his daughter was a sound sleeper who almost never woke up once she went down.

At twelve thirty, Dallas walked into the waiting room. "Any word?" he asked.

"I'm still waiting to speak to the doctor," Lucas said as Dallas sat in the chair next to him.

"If it's any consolation, she walked away from the wreck," Dallas said.

"She did?" Hope suddenly buoyed up inside Lucas.

"I swear, man. It was like a miracle. The car is completely totaled. Thankfully, she was wearing her seat belt. Still, I was concerned about internal injuries and that it was pure adrenaline that allowed her to crawl out of the wreckage and be on her feet."

"So what exactly happened? You told me she rolled her car. Did she fall asleep at the wheel or what?"

"She told me a truck rammed into the back of her. Unfortunately, she couldn't tell me a make or model. She couldn't even tell me the color. We were able to figure out some things by the wreckage the other car left behind."

Lucas's head reeled with this new information. "So somebody did this to her on purpose?" His blood chilled at the very thought, and instantly he thought about the note she had received.

"She wasn't sure. She thought maybe the driver of the other vehicle was drunk or high. She said the other driver was weaving all over the road before crashing into her. Whoever it was, they didn't stick around. Clive Burns was driving home from a friend's place and came upon the wreck. He's the one who called me."

"Thank God for Clive," Lucas said.

"We managed to pick up some pieces from the wreck that indicated the offending vehicle was black, and it will be missing part of a headlight. So I'll be checking with the garage to see if anyone brings in a black vehicle for headlight repair."

Their conversation halted as Dr. Erickson came out. Lucas jumped out of his chair. "How is she?" he immediately asked.

"She's banged up quite a bit. But I've run a battery of tests to make sure there's no internal damage, and everything checked out okay. Still, she suffered a trauma, and I'm keeping her overnight for observation."

"Can I see her?" Lucas asked.

The doctor nodded. "She's in room two. I've given her a mild sedative, so keep it brief."

"I'll go with you," Dallas said.

Together the two men walked out the door that would lead them into the hospital hallway. Thank God the doctor had said she had no internal injuries.

As Lucas stepped into room two, his heart constricted at the sight of her. The room was dim, with only a night-light above her head shining down on her.

Her eyes were closed, and she looked small in the hospital bed. She was hooked up to an IV bag and a blood pressure cuff that wasn't working at the moment.

Her eyes suddenly opened. "Lucas." She smiled for a second, and then her smile began to falter and tears filled her eyes.

"Hey…don't cry." He hurried over to the chair next to her bed and sat down. "Are you in pain? Do you need me to get the doctor?"

She shook her head and swiped at her tears. As she did, he saw a large blossoming bruise on her upper arm. "I just don't understand what happened." She looked at Dallas. "Does this have something to do with the note I received? Has Kenny found me and made his attacks on me in person? What is happening?" Her teary gaze went from Dallas to Lucas and then back to Dallas again.

"I can tell you with relative certainty that it isn't Kenny," Dallas replied. "I was planning on telling you both this tomorrow. I made contact with an officer in St. Louis who did some checking on Kenny. He was nowhere near here the night the note was left for you. In fact, he's a rather mild-mannered accountant who hasn't missed a day of work in the last fifteen years. He apparently only becomes Kenny the Creep when he's alone in front of his computer. The officer did us a favor and warned Kenny to have no more contact with you."

"So if not Kenny…then who?" She rubbed a hand across her forehead as if suffering from a severe headache. "Maybe it really was a drunk driver. The truck was definitely weaving all over the road before it hit me."

"Mary, you just rest and leave the investigation to me," Dallas said. Even though Dallas said the words with confidence, Lucas saw the exhaustion on his friend's face. Dallas was still dealing with trying to find out who had planted a human scarecrow in Lucas's cornfield. He asked Mary a few more questions about the accident, and then he left.

Once Dallas was gone, Lucas pulled Mary's hand into his. "Mary, I don't want you to worry about anything. I'll be here to pick you up tomorrow or whenever you get released, and you'll go back to my place and rest for as long as you need to."

"Maybe I should just quit working for you, Lucas. I'm more trouble than I'm worth," she said miserably. New tears shone in her eyes.

"Nonsense. I won't even entertain that kind of thinking." He gave her hand a light squeeze. "You're part of my family now, Mary. You can't bail on us now." He released her hand and stood. "Now, get some rest, and I'll see you tomorrow."

Once Lucas was back in his truck, he rested his forehead for several moments on the steering wheel as waves of emotion swept through him.

Thank God it appeared she was going to be just fine. Still, his worry wasn't completely waylaid. Somebody had hit her and caused a wreck that could have killed her. Had it been an accident? A drunk driver out of control? Or had it been on purpose?

He raised his head and stared out into the darkness of the night that had suddenly invaded his brain.

He tightened his hands on his steering wheel. If the crash had been on purpose, then it had definitely been a murder attempt.

Chapter 8

Mary awakened to sunshine drifting in through the hospital window in her room. Good grief, she felt as if she'd been run over by a truck...a very big truck. Every bone and muscle in her body hurt, but ultimately, she welcomed the pain. It told her she was alive.

She'd definitely thought she was going to die last night. When her car left the road and began to roll, up became down and down became up, and she'd truly believed she was going to be killed. It had been the most terrifying thing she'd ever been through.

She released a shuddery breath and closed her eyes once again. She was incredibly lucky. When the car had finally come to rest, her door was crushed closed, but she'd managed to crawl out of her broken window.

Immediately, she'd gotten out of the car and walked toward the road. She had no idea where her purse with her cell phone was in the car to call for help. She'd sat in the middle of the road, hoping and praying that somebody who could help her would appear.

Thankfully, Clive Burns had come along and had not only called Dallas, but he'd also insisted she sit in his car until help came.

She now opened her eyes at the sound of somebody entering her room. It was Amber James, one of the nurses. Mary knew her because the two had gone to high school together.

"Hi, Mary," Amber said with a bright smile. She was a pretty woman with shoulder-length brown hair and blue eyes. "How's our patient this morning?"

"Bones and muscles I didn't know I possessed are now screaming," Mary replied.

Amber smiled sympathetically. "I'm so sorry, Mary. But, according to what I heard, you are a very lucky woman."

"That, I agree with."

"You're also in luck because I have orders to give you something to help you with your pain. I'm just going to put it in your IV, and you should feel some relief within minutes," Amber said. "But before I do that, I need to get your vitals."

A few minutes later, Amber was gone, and as the pain relief took hold, Mary drifted back to sleep. She awakened again when breakfast arrived, followed closely by Dr. Erickson.

"Good morning, Mary," he said. "I'll bet you're feeling a bit rough today."

She smiled. "That's an understatement. Although, whatever Amber gave me earlier helped some."

"My shift is ending, so I wanted to let you know that you'll be in good hands with Dr. Reeves. I've caught him up on everything that's happened, and he should be in to see you later this morning."

"Can I go home today?" she asked.

"I see no reason why you can't be released later today," he said. "I'll make sure we send you home with a prescription for some pain pills. You're going to need to take it easy for a few days. You have been through a trauma. And all this is only if Dr. Reeves is in agreement."

She nodded. Thank goodness it was Sunday, her day off. She could go home, get into bed and watch television. If she could rest up today, then she should be fine by tomorrow to get back to her usual duties.

"Now, eat your breakfast and relax." Dr. Erickson smiled at her. "You are a very lucky woman to be with us today."

Once the doctor left her room, she ate some of the scrambled eggs and toast that had been delivered and then sipped on her coffee.

She'd have to make an insurance claim on her car; hopefully, she could get a rental. She wasn't sure if

O'Brian's Garage and Car Sales—the only car place in town—even kept rental cars.

She groaned inwardly when she thought of her purse. Would it be recovered from the accident? If it wasn't recovered, then she'd have to get a driver's license replacement, and she'd also have to call to check on her credit card and various other things. Would she even have a phone to make those calls?

Amber came back into her room. "If you're finished with your breakfast, then I can get that tray out of your way."

"I'm finished, thank you," Mary replied.

"Did that pain medication help you?"

"Yes, it did help a little."

"Good. I'll be back later," she said as she picked up the tray and then disappeared from the room.

When she left, Mary's thoughts turned to Lucas. Last night, he'd held her hand and told her she was part of his family. While both those things had warmed her, she wondered if he really thought she was more trouble than she was worth. First the note and now this. She'd know how he felt later today when she was released and he picked her up.

It was just after lunch when Dr. Ralph Reeves stopped by her room. The older man had been Mary's personal doctor through most of her life. He was a kind man who inspired trust and respect.

"Mary, from what I've heard, you're a very lucky lady," he said as he sat in the chair next to her bed. "How are you feeling this afternoon?"

"Like I've been run over by a very big truck," she said honestly.

He smiled sympathetically. "Unfortunately, you're probably going to feel that way for several days. You've been bruised up and banged around, and it's going to take some time for you to heal. Thank goodness you managed to escape with no broken bones or internal injuries."

"Can I go home?"

"There's really no reason to keep you here," he replied. "Do you feel ready to go home?"

"Absolutely." She could hurt in her room at Lucas's or here in the hospital. She'd rather be home.

"Then I'll work on the paperwork to get you out of here. You should be ready to go in the next half an hour or so." Dr. Reeves got to his feet, his pale blue eyes infinitely kind as he gazed at her. "Mary, be good to yourself, and take the time you need to heal."

"I will," she replied.

The minute the doctor left her room, she picked up the phone receiver in her room and punched in Lucas's number. He answered on the first ring.

"Mary, how are you doing?" There was a wealth of concern in his voice, and for a moment she felt like crying.

"I'm doing okay," she replied and swallowed hard against her tears. "In fact, I'm going to be released in about a half an hour or so."

"Annabelle and I will be there," he said. "We'll see you when we get there."

"Thank you, Lucas."

Tears once again pressed hot behind her eyes as she hung up the phone. What in the heck was wrong with her? She knew the answer. She was hurting all over, and the pain made her more emotional than she'd ever been. She had to get her emotions under control before Lucas and Annabelle arrived.

Fifteen minutes later, Amber came back. "I've got your paperwork all ready to go," she said. "Your clothes are in the closet. Do you need help getting dressed?"

"No, I can manage," Mary replied.

"Then I'll take out your IV and help you out of bed."

Minutes later, Mary sat on the edge of the bed. Her blouse and jeans were ruined. They were grass- and oil-stained, and her jeans now had rips in the legs. Amber gave her the paperwork, along with a prescription for pain pills.

Mary heard Annabelle before she saw her. Despite her pain, the sound of those little footsteps and giggles coming down the hallway made her smile.

She whirled into Mary's room and then halted with Lucas just behind her. "Ms. Mary, we got you flowers." Lucas held out an arrangement of beautiful, colorful flowers.

"That was very nice of you," Mary replied.

"Daddy told me you have lots of boo-boos." The little girl sidled up to Mary. "Oh, I see a boo-boo."

She pointed to the bruise on Mary's upper arm. "Want me to kiss it better?"

Mary's heart expanded. Annabelle looked so serious and so caring. "Maybe a kiss would make it much better." She leaned down so Annabelle could give her a soft kiss on the bruise.

"I misted you, Ms. Mary," Annabelle said.

"We both missed you." Lucas cleared his throat and smiled at Mary. "I spoke to Dr. Erickson earlier this morning, and he told me you were doing well, but you were in a lot of pain."

"That's about the sum of it," she replied. Before she could say anything more, Amber appeared in the doorway with a wheelchair.

"Are we ready to go?" she asked brightly.

"I'm ready," Mary said.

"Ready," Annabelle echoed and clapped her hands together. "Daddy, give Ms. Mary her flowers." Lucas handed Mary the flower arrangement.

"Annabelle and I will pull up the truck at the emergency room entrance," Lucas said. "Come on, Annabelle."

The two left together. "What a sweetheart," Amber said of Annabelle. "She's absolutely beautiful and seems so bright."

"She is all that and more," Mary said as she sat in the wheelchair. The scent of the flowers filled the air, and Mary was touched that Lucas had gone to the trouble of buying them for her.

"I hope you feel better with each day that passes,"

Amber said. She pushed Mary out of the room and down the hallway.

"Thank you for taking such good care of me," Mary replied.

"It was my pleasure."

They left the hospital and went out into the hot afternoon. Lucas's truck was at the curb, and he quickly got out of the driver's seat and hurried around to where she was getting out of the wheelchair. He opened the passenger door and then gently took her arm to help her up and into the truck.

After saying goodbye to Amber, they were on their way. "Ms. Mary, you play with me?" Annabelle asked from her car seat in the back.

"Ms. Mary can't play today," Lucas said before Mary could reply. "Ms. Mary is going to rest, and we're going to take care of her."

"I take care of her," Annabelle said. "I take care of her 'cause I love Ms. Mary."

"Oh, honey. I love you, too," Mary replied, her heart melting at the little girl's words despite the pain that racked her body.

"We'll drive through the pharmacy and get that prescription filled before heading home," Lucas said.

"Thank you. I really appreciate it." She was ready for whatever pain pill the doctor had prescribed. It seemed like a long time ago that she'd gotten a little relief from whatever had been in her IV.

They got the pills and then headed back to the farm. Mary tried not to worry about any consequence the accident might bring up. If she couldn't get a rental car, then she'd have to rely on Lucas to get to the store whenever she needed to go.

Was she really worth this kind of trouble to him? Wouldn't it just be easier for him to hire somebody who didn't get strange notes and didn't wreck their car? Somebody who required far less work than her?

"If you'd like, we can put you here on the sofa rather than in your room," Lucas said when they were inside the house. He placed the flower arrangement on the end table.

"That would be nice," she replied. Even though she'd first believed she wanted to be in her room, she'd been alone with her thoughts all day, and now isolating in her room didn't sound so good.

"Why don't you go change into something more comfortable?" he suggested.

Mary nodded and headed down the hall to her bedroom. Once there, the first thing she saw was her purse on the bed. She checked inside and breathed a sigh of relief. Everything seemed to be there. She took out her cell phone, which was dead, and plugged it in to charge.

She then took off her clothes and tossed them on the floor to be thrown away later. She was sporting a large bruise on one hip and several more down one leg. *No wonder I hurt*, she thought as she changed into an oversize T-shirt and a pair of comfortable shorts.

When she returned to the living room, she eased

down into a sitting position on the sofa. "I saw my purse," she said.

"Yeah, Dallas brought it by earlier this morning."

"Thank goodness. Now I don't have to go to the hassle of replacing anything," she replied.

"I said to get comfortable. Go ahead and stretch out, Mary," Lucas encouraged her. "I'll bring you a pillow and a blanket." He disappeared down the hallway.

"I'll get you a pillow," Annabelle said and raced for her bedroom. She returned a moment later with a decorative pillow shaped like a heart. "This is my mostest favorite pillow," she said and gave it to Mary.

"Thank you, honey. How about if I hold it in my lap?" she said as Lucas returned with a bed pillow and a soft, fluffy beige blanket.

He placed the pillow behind her head and then covered her with the blanket. "Are you ready for one of those pain pills?"

"Oh, yes, I am." She started to sit up, but Lucas waved her back down.

"I'll get one for you." He went into the kitchen and returned a moment later with one of the pills and a glass of water.

"Lucas, I don't want you to wait on me," she protested.

"Nonsense. Annabelle and I intend to take very good care of you. Right, Annabelle?"

"Right," Annabelle replied and then raced back into her bedroom.

"Remember that movie we talked about wanting to see the other night?" Lucas asked. "The comedy about the hapless taxman in a small town in Kentucky?"

"I remember," she replied.

"How about we watch it now?"

"Sounds good to me."

"Are you sure you're comfortable?" Lucas asked. There was no mistaking the warmth and caring in his gaze, and it definitely shot a warmth through her.

Annabelle came running out of her room, a baby doll tucked beneath her arm. "Here, Ms. Mary. This is Baby Nurse. If you hold her, then you will feel better."

She handed the doll over and then leaned her head against Mary and patted her side. "Poor Ms. Mary."

A new wave of emotion washed over Mary. This didn't feel like a job. It felt like more—much more—than a job…even though she knew it was an illusion she shouldn't buy into. The truth was that, right at this very moment, this felt like a family. It felt like *her* family.

Despite Mary's protests, Lucas didn't go out in the fields on Monday. He knew Mary was still stiff and sore, and he also knew she wouldn't take any of her pain pills if she was alone with Annabelle.

Another day of rest was what she needed, and he insisted she do just that. She'd already contacted her insurance company about the wreck and her need of a rental car. Arrangements were being made to get her what she needed.

Annabelle was proving to be a good little nurse. She played quietly in the living room, and every fifteen minutes or so, she'd run to Mary's side and stroke her arm or her face and ask her what she needed. It warmed his heart to see his daughter show such compassion and caring at her young age. It was also evident just how much she loved her Ms. Mary.

It was two in the afternoon when Nicole stopped by. Annabelle was napping, and Lucas and Mary had been watching another movie.

"Oh, Mary, my dear. How are you feeling?" Nicole asked as she came into the living room.

"A little better today," Mary replied. She shifted to a sitting position, leaving room for Nicole to sit next to her.

"Lucas told me what happened. It must have been absolutely terrifying for you. You are a very lucky woman."

Mary laughed. "If I had a quarter for everyone who has said that to me since the accident, I'd be wealthy."

As always, Lucas was struck by the beauty of her smile, by the melodious sound of her laughter. He wished he could take away the pain he knew she still felt from the accident. He wished he could take her in his arms and… He suddenly realized Nicole was looking at him and apparently waiting for a response.

"I'm sorry—what did you say?" he asked Nicole.

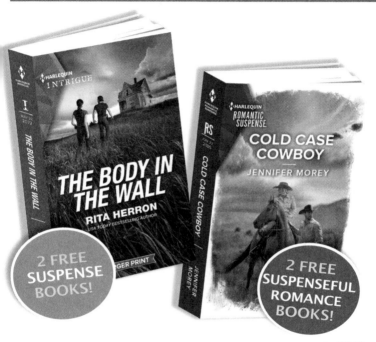

YOU pick your books – WE pay for everything.
You get up to FOUR New Books and TWO Mystery Gifts...absolutely FREE!

Dear Reader,

I am writing to announce the launch of a huge **FREE BOOKS GIVEAWAY**... and to let you know that YOU are entitled to choose up to FOUR fantastic books that WE pay for.

Try **Harlequin® Romantic Suspense** books featuring heart-racing page-turners with unexpected plot twists and irresistible chemistry that will keep you guessing to the very end.

Try **Harlequin Intrigue® Larger-Print** books featuring action-packed stories that will keep you on the edge of your seat. Solve the crime and deliver justice at all costs.

Or TRY BOTH!

In return, we ask just one favor: Would you please participate in our brief Reader Survey? We'd love to hear from you.

This FREE BOOKS GIVEAWAY means that your introductory shipment is completely free, <u>even the shipping</u>! If you decide to continue, you can look forward to curated monthly shipments of brand-new books from your selected series, always at a discount off the cover price! <u>Plus you can cancel any time</u>. Who could pass up a deal like that?

Sincerely

Pam Powers

Pam Powers
For Harlequin Reader Service

Complete the survey below and return it today to receive up to 4 FREE BOOKS and FREE GIFTS guaranteed!

▲ If offer card is missing write to: Harlequin Reader Service, P.O. Box 1341, Buffalo, NY 14240-8531 or visit www.ReaderService.com ▲

BUSINESS REPLY MAIL
FIRST-CLASS MAIL   PERMIT NO. 717   BUFFALO, NY

POSTAGE WILL BE PAID BY ADDRESSEE

HARLEQUIN READER SERVICE
PO BOX 1341
BUFFALO NY 14240-8571

NO POSTAGE
NECESSARY
IF MAILED
IN THE
UNITED STATES

"I said maybe I'll take Annabelle for an overnight with Granny tonight. She hasn't spent the night with me for a while, and with Mary laid up, it's a perfect opportunity."

"Please don't feel obligated on my account," Mary protested. "I'm getting along just fine."

"Still, I think I need a granddaughter fix," Nicole replied.

"Well, in that case, why don't you come back right after dinner and pick her up? Or I can drop her off at your place," Lucas suggested. "That way, I can feed her and pack a little bag for her."

"Sounds perfect," Nicole agreed. "I'll just come pick her up." She got up from the sofa. "Oh, I almost forgot." She reached into her purse and pulled out a photo. "I found this when I was cleaning out a drawer, and I thought you might like it."

Lucas took the photo from her—a picture of him and Diana on Nicole's back porch. It instantly evoked feelings of grief and a bit of guilt that he didn't want to examine too closely.

"I just thought it was a wonderful picture of Diana," Nicole said.

"It is a good picture of her," he agreed.

"Oh, Lucas. She loved you so much. Anyway, I thought you might want to frame that and put it on the little accent table by the front door."

"Thanks, Nicole."

"You're welcome. And now I'm off. I'll be back for the munchkin around five."

Lucas walked her out, and as soon as she was out the front door, he tucked the picture into the drawer of the accent table. Nicole often brought him photos of Diana. It was as if she feared he would forget her daughter. But he would never forget the wife he'd loved...the mother of his beloved daughter.

It wasn't long after she left that Annabelle woke up, and she and Lucas built towers with her blocks while Mary cheered them on.

He stopped the games long enough to make dinner. He kept it simple: hot dogs and chips. Once they were finished eating, he told Annabelle that her grandma was coming to pick her up for a sleepover.

Annabelle was delighted, and after the kitchen was clean, Lucas took his daughter to her room to pack her overnight bag. They had just finished with that when Nicole returned.

After sending them on their way, he came back to the living room, where Mary was seated on the sofa. He sank down in his recliner and released a deep sigh. "The house seems to lose a lot of its energy when Annabelle isn't here."

Mary smiled. "I was just thinking the same thing. Even when she's sleeping, she's a presence in the house."

"She's definitely grown very attached to you," he observed.

"Does that bother you?" Mary asked, her voice filled with concern.

"No, it doesn't bother me at all. In fact, I'm glad

she loves you and that you can be a strong female presence in her life. She needs that. It's something I can't give her."

"I can tell you honestly that I'm crazy in love with her, too. She is such an amazing little girl, and she has such a sweet heart." She frowned. "There's only one little area of concern I have for her."

Lucas sat up straighter in his chair. "What's that?" he asked in alarm.

Mary laughed. "Calm down, papa bear. It's nothing too serious."

"Whew. You had me worried for a minute. So, what's the area of concern?"

"Annabelle plays very well with me, and she plays very well with you, but this is usually about the time when children learn to socialize with other children. The whole time I've been here, she hasn't mentioned having little friends."

"That's because she doesn't have any," Lucas admitted.

"I think it's important for her to get socialized with other children before she starts school. Do you know anyone in town who has a child or children around her age?"

He frowned thoughtfully. "I've got a couple of friends who have kids her age."

"Would you mind if I set up a playdate with them?"

"I wouldn't mind it at all, but let's talk about it when you're feeling a little bit better," he replied.

It felt good to be sitting here with her and talking about Annabelle. It felt as if they were two concerned parents discussing their child.

And with that came that unexpected kick of desire for her. There was a growing closeness between them he couldn't deny. Once again, he realized he wouldn't feel this for just any woman. It was specific to Mary.

"You'd better not try to stay out of the fields tomorrow," she now said. "I'm feeling well enough to take care of things around here, and I would hate to embarrass you by kicking you out of your own home in the morning."

"Ha. You and what army?" he replied teasingly.

"I don't need an army," she said, her eyes sparkling brightly. "I have secret skills."

He laughed. "What kind of secret skills?"

"Well, now, if I told you, they wouldn't be secret."

He found her sexy as hell at this moment, with her eyes shining and her lips curved into a teasing smile. She was easy to banter with, and that made him want to get even closer to her.

"On a more serious note, I wanted to tell you that I wavered over calling your parents to let them know about the accident. Of course, in the end, I knew it wasn't my place," he said.

"Thank goodness you didn't call them. If you had, they would have worried that I might need or want something from them." Even though her tone was unemotional, he sensed the pain behind the words.

And he hurt for her. What must it be like to grow up in a place where there was no warmth, no support… no love? Mary had to be incredibly strong to survive that kind of upbringing and still be as loving and as open as she was. It was a testament to her character… to her very soul.

As they continued to talk about everything and anything, he couldn't escape the desire that continued to fire heat through his veins.

It was just after seven when a knock fell on his front door. "Maybe Annabelle turned out to be too much for Nicole," he said as he got out of his chair to answer.

It wasn't Nicole. It was Gina Hightower. The dark-haired woman smiled. "Hi, Lucas. I was just driving by and decided to stop in to get my pot back from you."

"Oh, yeah. I have it in the kitchen. Come on in, and I'll get it for you," he replied.

As he hurried to the kitchen and grabbed the pot, he heard Gina greet Mary. He returned to the living room, where Gina was questioning Mary about the accident.

"So, you really have no idea who hit you?" Gina asked.

"I know it was a black pickup truck, but that's all," Mary replied.

"Unfortunately, black pickup trucks are a dime a dozen around here," Gina said.

Mary nodded. "And that's a problem in finding the driver."

"So, Dallas hasn't figured out who was driving yet?"

"Not that we've heard about," Lucas said.

"Ah, that looks like my pot," Gina said to him.

He smiled. "This would be your pot." He handed it to her.

"Then I'll just get on my way." She grinned at Mary. "Mary, I hope you feel better soon." She turned back to Lucas. "Walk me out?"

"I'll be right back," he said to Mary, and then he and Gina left the house.

"Beautiful evening," he observed as they walked toward the driveway.

"Still a little warm for me," she replied. When they reached her car, she put the pot in the back seat, and then she turned to face him. "You know, Lucas, I'd be far better for you than her."

He started to protest and tell her that things weren't that way between him and Mary. But before he got a chance, Gina continued.

"I know how much you loved Diana, but she's gone, Lucas. She's been gone for a long time now. You're still a young man with a lot of life left to live. A dead woman can't fill your evenings with conversation. She can't rub your back when your muscles are sore. She can't warm your bed in the winter or make love to you all year long."

She flipped a strand of her dark hair over her

shoulder as her gaze held his intently. "Lucas, I could do all those things for you, and I'm right here and alive. I could be a loving stepmother to Annabelle. I could give her the hugs and kisses that her dead mother can't give to her. You don't need Mary to take care of her. You'd have me."

"Gina..." he began.

She leaned forward and placed her index finger against his lips. "You don't have to say anything right now. Just think about what I've said." She opened her driver's-side door and slid into the car. "Good night, Lucas."

He stood and watched until her car disappeared from sight. He was almost offended by her words—by her just assuming she was better for him than the memories of his wife.

He would have been completely offended if he hadn't been entertaining some of those very same things deep inside his heart. Only it certainly wasn't Gina he thought about when his mind drifted into that kind of dangerous territory.

Mary. It was Mary who filled his evenings with conversation and laughter. It was Mary who gave his daughter lots of kisses and hugs, who wiped her tears when she cried and giggled with her when she was happy.

Finally, it was Mary he wanted to kiss until they were both mindless. It was Mary he wanted to take to his bed and make slow, sweet love to.

However, he wasn't going to do that. He was going to fantasize about her and ache for her and try to keep things with her as professional as possible.

Chapter 9

Lucas instantly awakened, every muscle in his body tense. Had Annabelle cried out for him? No… no, that couldn't be right. Annabelle wasn't in her bed tonight. She was with Nicole. He relaxed back against the mattress and closed his eyes once again, assuming it might have been a dream that had awakened him.

Almost immediately, he heard it again…a cry of distress. Mary. He sat straight up. Was she in trouble? The note she'd received weeks before suddenly shot into his head. Somebody banging into her car… Had somebody somehow entered her room? Broken in through one of the windows? Was it somebody who wanted to harm her?

He jumped out of bed and left his bedroom. He hurried down the hall to her room. Standing outside the closed door, he hesitated. Then she cried out once again.

He threw open her door and instantly assessed what was going on. Moonlight drifted in through the windows, and Mary was thrashing in the bed, obviously in the throes of a bad nightmare.

Should he wake her? Or should he let her nightmare play out? When her thrashing intensified and he could see the sheen of tears falling from her closed eyes and her terrified cries became more frantic, he couldn't stand it anymore.

He moved to the side of her bed. "Mary? Mary, honey, wake up. You're having a nightmare." Her head twisted back and forth on the pillow as she continued to suffer whatever nightscape was in her mind.

Not wanting her to endure another moment longer, he sat on the edge of the bed and gently shook her shoulder. Her eyes snapped open, filled with terror. Then she focused in on him, and with a deep gasp, she launched herself into his arms.

He tightened his arms around her as she began to weep. "Scarecrows… They were everywhere… Ch-chasing me. I was…I was…in my car, and…and then I was r-rolling upside down a-and downside up, and…and the scarecrows k-kept coming." Her words came out with tearful gasps as she buried her face against his bare shoulder.

"Shhh, you're okay now," he murmured against her ear as he patted her slender back. "You're safe here. It was just a bad dream."

She wrapped her arms more tightly around his neck. Despite her tears, he was acutely aware of her warm body intimately close to his. He could feel the press of her full breasts against his bare chest, smell the scent of her that always stirred him on a primal level.

Still, his desire was to comfort her and nothing more. He held her until her weeping finally stopped. She lingered in his arms for several minutes longer and then unwound her arms from around his neck.

She leaned back from him, her face whitewashed by the silver moonlight that poured through the window. "I'm sorry. I'm so sorry." She covered her face with her hands. "I'm so embarrassed."

"Why on earth would you be embarrassed?" He gently pulled her hands away from her face. "Mary, you had a nightmare. From what you said, it must have been a bad one. There's nothing to be embarrassed about."

She gazed at him, the fear in her eyes ebbing away and being replaced with something else—something that made his breath catch in the back of his throat.

"Thank you, Lucas, for waking me up," she finally said and leaned toward him, her lips slightly parted as if in invitation.

Get up. Get off the bed. The voice whispered in his head with a ringing alarm. *Get away from her.*

However, it was as if his head and his body were disconnected from each other.

"Lucas." She whispered his name with what sounded like longing.

At that moment, his brain quit working. He gathered her back into his arms and took her lips with his own. Instantly, her arms wrapped around his neck as she once again opened her mouth to him.

His tongue swirled with hers as white-hot desire coursed through his veins. It felt as if he'd wanted this—he'd wanted Mary—forever. She'd been a burn in his blood and a fire in his gut for so long.

As she leaned even closer, he again felt the press of her breasts against his skin, although this time, he felt the pebbled hardness of her nipples through the material of her nightshirt. That only increased his desire for her.

When the kiss finally ended, they stared at each other. Should he apologize now and get the hell out of her room? He should do that, but it was the very last thing he wanted.

Still, their gazes remained locked, and he could swear he saw a hunger in the depths of her eyes. He didn't move. "Lucas, I…I want you." The words whispered out of her.

He groaned. "Oh, Mary, I want you, too."

He knew it was wrong. He knew they were crossing a line that might forever change the dynamics of their relationship. But she made him weak. She made him not want to think rationally. He didn't even want to think about the consequences at this moment.

He took her back in his arms and lowered her onto the mattress. At the same time, he moved onto the bed next to her. His lips captured hers once again in a fiery kiss.

His hands stroked up and down her back as the kiss continued. He had to remember to be gentle. She was bruised all over, and the last thing he wanted to do was hurt her. When the kiss ended, she pushed him away, and he instantly pulled back from her.

"Mary, you can say no at any time and I'll go back to my room," he said half-breathlessly. "I know you must be still hurting, and the last thing I want is to cause you any pain."

"Oh, Lucas, I don't want to say no," she replied with a soft smile. "I'm saying yes."

To his surprise, she moved beneath the sheet and then pulled her nightshirt over her head and tossed it onto the end of the bed.

She covered her bare breasts with her hands, but he pulled her hands away. "Don't hide yourself, Mary. You are so beautiful."

"You make me feel beautiful," she replied. Her eyes gleamed a vivid green that he wanted to fall into and drown.

He reached for her once again. Their mouths crashed together, and his hands covered her breasts. Her skin was so soft…so wonderfully warm. She moaned as his fingers teased her nipples, and the sound of her pleasure only made him hotter for her. He wanted to please her like no man before him ever had. He wanted to satisfy her like no other man would ever do.

As he stroked down the length of her body, she kissed his neck, behind his ear. It was as if she knew every place that would bring him even more pleasure.

He caressed along her side and down her thigh. He loved touching her. It had been so long—so very long—since he'd felt this wonderfully alive.

His hand finally reached the very center of her. He swept his hand across her silky underwear, and she arched up to meet his touch.

The silk was hot and damp, and it wasn't long before he wanted it off her. She was obviously of the same mind. As he tugged at the underwear, she raised herself up to aid him.

Once she was completely naked, he took off his boxers. She reached down and encircled his throbbing hardness with her fingers. As she moved her hand up and down, the sensations nearly sent him over the edge.

He was on fire. His heart beat so fast, so frantically, he could hear it in his head. It was all her... all Mary. He was positively drowning in her. He finally had to push her hand away. Instead, he moved between her legs, and she welcomed him.

He hovered over her for a long moment, losing himself in the simmering depths of her eyes. He slowly eased into her, and the warmth and tightness of her surrounding him momentarily stole his breath away.

He began to thrust his hips forward and back, moving inside her with slow, steady strokes. She grabbed hold of his buttocks and urged him deeper and deeper inside her.

Lost. He was completely lost in her. His brain no longer worked. He had no more thoughts. It was all Mary and the sweet and hot sensations she evoked in him.

As she met him thrust for thrust, her breaths came faster, her movements wilder, and then she was there, moaning deep and long as her climax washed over her.

Once he knew she had been pleasured, he lost all control. He surged inside her as his own climax pulsated out of him. He groaned her name as his release crashed through him.

He finally rolled over onto his side as he waited for his breathing to return to normal. "Did I hurt you?" he finally asked, thinking about her bruising from the accident.

"No, not at all," she replied. "Lucas?" She hesitated a moment. "Could you stay here with me for the rest of the night?"

He thought about the nightmare she had suffered and wondered if she was afraid it might come back again. "Yes, I'll stay here with you tonight," he replied. "I'll be right back."

He got up from the bed and grabbed his boxers from where he'd tossed them on the floor. He then left the bedroom and went into the bathroom in his own room.

He refused to look at himself in the mirror. The first stirrings of self-recriminations were trying to take hold of him, and he was afraid to see that in his eyes, on his face.

He didn't want to think about how wrong making love to Mary had been. Damn, it had been so crazy, so unexpected, they hadn't even used birth control. How stupid had that been? It just proved how he hadn't been thinking at all.

Still, he'd worry about all that tomorrow in the light of day. Right now, all he wanted to do was think about how wonderful it had been with her. He'd fantasized about making love to her for weeks, and she had definitely lived up to the fantasy.

She'd been so soft and warm, so eager and willing. She'd been so alive and passionate. Just thinking about it made him want to make love to her all over again.

He pulled his boxers back on and then returned to her bedroom. She was once again in her nightshirt. When he got back into the bed, she immediately snuggled up against him. He wrapped his arm around her and marveled at how neatly she fit against him.

"Thank you for staying here with me," she said.

"I don't mind," he replied. "I just want you to feel safe as you fall back asleep. I'm right here if a nightmare tries to take hold of you again, and I'll wake you up immediately."

She was silent for several minutes, and he wondered if she'd fallen back asleep. "Lucas," she said softly, letting him know she was still awake.

"Yeah?"

"It was wonderful."

He tightened his arm around her. "Yes, it was. Now, it's late. Go to sleep."

"Night, Lucas."

"Good night, Mary."

Her breathing became slow and even, and he knew she had fallen asleep. It felt good to have her next to him as he sought his own slumber. He'd forgotten how nice it was to hold somebody in his arms through the night.

He matched his breathing to hers and tried to go to sleep. But sleep wouldn't come. Instead, thoughts of Diana filled his head. This had been a dishonor to her memory. He'd vowed to always love her, and now he held another woman in his arms.

Despite how wonderful it had been to make love with Mary, it now felt like a regrettable mistake. A moment of weakness that sent shame running through him.

A dead woman can't fill your evenings with conversation. She can't warm your bed in the winter or make love to you all year long. Gina's words played and replayed in his mind, further complicating his thoughts.

All he knew for sure was that, first thing in the morning, he and Mary needed to talk. He had to make sure she understood that this could never—*would* never—happen again.

Mary awoke to find herself in bed alone. The pillow next to hers was still warm, letting her know Lucas hadn't left that long ago.

She wasn't eager to jump up and get out of bed. She wanted to take a few minutes and think about the night she had shared with Lucas.

If she hadn't had the nightmare, then none of it would have happened. As horrible as the nightmare had been, she was almost glad it *had* happened, since it had brought her a magical night with Lucas.

And it had been magical. Lucas had been the kind of lover she'd only dreamed about. He'd been passionate and masterful and yet giving and tender. He'd made her feel incredibly wanted and beautiful.

Her body tingled now just thinking about it. Still, she had no idea how this might change things between them. She hoped they could keep this closeness, this intimacy, going without any complications arising in their professional roles.

After all, they were two consenting adults, and what they did together in the nighttime was nobody else's business. But these feelings she had for Lucas weren't just about what they had shared the night before.

Her feelings had grown from the evenings when

they talked and laughed together. Her feelings had come from the hours of watching him interact with his daughter.

She liked the way he smelled—like sunshine and warm breezes. She respected how hard he worked at providing a good life for his daughter and everyone else in his life. He was a thoughtful, intelligent man. She also knew he was well respected and well-liked in the community.

The truth of the matter was she was in love with him. It wasn't just a silly crush anymore. It was the love of a woman for her man. He was her person. He was the man she'd like to build dreams with and see those dreams come true.

However, she was also realistic enough to know that just because he was her person, that didn't mean she was *his* person. This could have heartache written all over it. If he rebuffed her after last night, he would never know how deeply she'd be hurt.

She would continue to do her job to the best of her ability. She would support him and pour her love into Annabelle. She would be able to keep working for him without him ever knowing her true feelings.

She finally pulled herself out of bed and into the shower.

The bruises on her body had grown deeper and darker, but she knew they would eventually fade and go away. She had gotten through yesterday without taking any pain pills, and she had no intention or need to take any more.

Dressing in a pair of jeans and a green-and-white-striped tank top, she wondered how awkward things might be between them when he got home from work today.

There was no way to know until she faced him. With this thought in mind, she left her bedroom and followed the scent of fresh coffee into the kitchen.

Lucas was seated at the table. "Good morning," he said.

"You aren't supposed to be here," she said. "You're supposed to be out in the fields working today." She smiled at him. "And a good morning to you, too." She got herself a cup of coffee and then sat across from him.

"I decided to give you one more day of rest today," he replied.

"You know you didn't have to do that."

"I know I didn't have to, but I wanted to. Did you sleep well?" he asked. She sensed a faint distance in his gaze.

"When I eventually got back to sleep, I slept like a baby." What she wanted to tell him was that she'd slept like a baby because his arms had surrounded her, making her feel loved and protected through the night.

"About last night…" He frowned and Mary steeled herself for whatever he was about to say. His gaze shot away from her before he looked at her once again.

"Mary, about last night. You know that shouldn't

have happened between us. I...I don't even have an excuse other than I was weak. It was a huge mistake, and it will never happen again. I loved my wife... I still love my wife, and all I need from you is what you've been doing by being my nanny and housekeeper."

Each and every word he said sliced straight through to the center of her heart. He spoke without emotion, as if ordering off the menu at the café. Last night, it had felt like he'd made love to her; this morning, he was making her feel like she'd just been a convenient sex partner.

"Hell, Mary, we didn't even use birth control," he said.

"That shouldn't be a problem. I'm on the pill," she replied. "Lucas, you're making a far bigger deal about this than it has to be. We're two consenting adults, and what happened between us last night happened. But nothing has changed. I'm still your housekeeper and nanny."

He breathed an audible sigh of relief and finally smiled at her. "Thanks, Mary...for understanding." His smile faltered. "I somehow lost my way last night. I feel guilty for forgetting momentarily how much I love Diana."

"Give yourself a break, Lucas. Last night, you were only human—and as you said, it won't happen again. Now, what can I fix you for breakfast?" She needed to get up from the table. She wanted to not think about the pain his words had caused her and get back to some semblance of a routine.

"How about I make you breakfast?" he asked.

"Absolutely not. It's Tuesday. You are supposed to be working, and I'm on duty, despite you believing I need another day off."

"Mary, I saw all your bruises last night. I know you must still be hurting. I want you to take it easy for the rest of the day, and tomorrow you can be back on duty." He rose from the table. "Now, what can I fix you for breakfast?"

"Anything is fine." Why did he have to be so nice to her? So caring? It would be so much easier for her if he wasn't—especially now, with her heart as bruised as the rest of her.

"Then I vote for some French toast." He grabbed the eggs out of the refrigerator and got to work.

As Mary watched him, she couldn't help the love for him that swelled her heart. And she couldn't fight against a dead woman's memory. Nobody could.

It was obvious he felt guilty about making love—no, *having sex*—with Mary. She suspected he felt as if he'd cheated on Diana. He would never love Mary the way she did him. All he wanted from her was housekeeping and childcare, and she could do that. Hopefully, her love for him would eventually die.

"When do you expect Nicole to bring Annabelle home?" she asked as they sat at the table, eating the French toast he'd made.

"When she keeps her overnight, she usually brings her home after lunch," he replied.

"Maybe today you could write down the names and numbers of people you know who have kids her age?"

"I can do that," he said. "But I still don't want you planning any playdates for at least a week. You still need to heal, Mary. It's only been three days ago that you wrecked and could have died."

His words brought back the horror of the accident, and for a moment, the terror of that night pressed tight against her chest. She took a drink of her coffee as the memories flooded through her.

"I just wish I knew if it was an accident or if somebody really was trying to kill me," she said as she placed her cup back on the table.

"The truck who rammed into you suffered front-end damage. I'm sure Dallas will be checking not only with the garage here but also the garages all around the area," Lucas replied. "He'll get the driver, Mary. I have a lot of faith in him as a good lawman."

"And yet he still hasn't been able to arrest somebody for Cindy's death." Mary fought back a shudder as a vision of the poor woman filled her head.

"He will. Eventually, he'll catch the bastard who did that to Cindy." He leaned back in his chair and released a rueful smile. "I have to say, our morning conversation so far has been pretty dark and dismal."

"I'm sorry," she replied.

He stared at her for a long moment, and in the

depths of his eyes, she could swear she saw a wealth of caring. "You have to stop apologizing for everything. These things aren't your fault, and you don't owe anyone an apology."

She flushed. "I'm s—" She stopped and then laughed. "I was about to do it again. I guess it's a lingering effect from my childhood. When people tell you everything bad that happens to them is somehow your fault, you learn to apologize even if you're not at fault. Now, you cooked, so I'll clean up the kitchen."

"Nonsense. You just sit tight and relax." He got up from the table and grabbed their plates.

"Lucas, I'm not an invalid," she protested. "I appreciate your kindness. But really, I'm fine."

"You can suffer me treating you like an invalid for one more day." He offered her one of his most charming smiles. "I'm your boss, and I insist you take this one more day off."

"Who am I to argue with the boss?" She returned his smile with one of her own.

Once again, Mary found herself resting on the sofa with the television playing. Lucas went into his office to make a couple of business phone calls, and then he returned to sit with her.

"I didn't even ask you if you had a good time at the Farmer's Club on Saturday night," she said.

"I did. It was a low-key night talking with some of the old-timers in the area. I always enjoy that, and I always learn something new from them. What about you? Did you have a good time at Murphy's before you made the drive back?"

"It was okay. I danced a few times and had a few laughs with the girls."

"Who did you dance with?" One of his dark brows rose curiously.

"Jeff Wyland and Ethan Dourty. They always ask me to dance when I'm at Murphy's and they are there," she replied.

"I don't know Jeff very well, but Ethan takes care of all my insurance needs. He seems like a good guy."

"They're both nice men."

The conversation slowly ebbed away, and they both turned their attention to the television. The silence between them grew. Mary couldn't think of anything to say to break the uncomfortable quiet, and apparently neither could he.

She hoped this didn't portend the way their relationship would now go. Even though she wouldn't take back what had happened between them the night before, she hoped it hadn't destroyed the warmth and caring and general great relationship they had shared up until that point.

There was a possibility the car accident had been an attempt to kill her because she was living here with Lucas. What might the culprit do if he or she knew they had made love?

The very thought shot a shiver up her spine.

Chapter 10

It had been over a week since Mary's accident, and Lucas was still struggling with the guilt he felt over making love with her. And what made matters worse was that he wanted her all over again. That want battled with his memories of Diana. But they were just memories.

He and Diana would never spend any more time together again. He would never hold her in his arms or make love to her again. All he had of her were those memories, and he was beginning to wonder if that was really enough to fill him up for the rest of his life.

He was working harder than ever in the fields, and when he was finished with that, he had also begun to clean out his barn. He was pushing himself to near exhaustion each day, hoping he would be too tired to think, to feel, by the time he went back into the house for dinner and faced Mary once again.

This evening was no different. As he trudged toward the house, he was hot and sweaty and dirty, and all he could think about was how fresh and clean and flowery Mary would smell.

Her scent now seemed to permeate every room in the house. He was acutely aware of every move she made when they were together. She fed him not only physically but emotionally as well. Dammit, if he was smart, he'd fire her and get her as far away from him as possible.

But how fair would that be to her? How fair would that be to Annabelle, who loved Ms. Mary with all her heart? How selfish would he be to fire her just because he couldn't control his own thoughts and his desires where she was concerned?

The simple truth of the matter was Mary made him happy. She'd made the house feel like a real home. He looked forward each evening to coming in after a hard day of work.

All these thoughts were roaring in his head as he stepped through the back door. The kitchen smelled wonderful, and both Mary and Annabelle greeted him with big smiles that shot straight through to his heart.

"Daddy!" Annabelle held out a picture she'd colored. "I drewed a picture for you."

He took it from her. There was a house, a huge sun and three stick figures. "Is this Mommy and Daddy and Annabelle?"

"No, Daddy. It's you and me and Ms. Mary," she replied.

"Well, it's a wonderful picture," he told her.

"Why don't I put it on the refrigerator with all the other works of art?" Mary said. She took the picture from him. "And dinner is ready whenever you are."

"The first thing I need to do is go take a hot shower. It will only take me a few minutes."

"Take as much time as you need. We'll be here when you're ready. Right, Annabelle?"

"Right!" she replied with a happy grin.

Lucas left the kitchen. Minutes later, he was standing beneath a hot spray of water. He didn't know why he'd asked Annabelle if Mommy was in the picture she'd drawn.

Annabelle didn't know "Mommy" at all. She had absolutely no memories of Diana. Even though he and Nicole had talked about Diana and how much she'd loved Annabelle, a three-year-old couldn't really understand the concept of a mother who wasn't present.

By the time he returned to the kitchen, he thought he had his emotions under control. "Now you can tell me what smells so good," he said as he sat at the table.

"Smothered chicken with noodles, broccoli with cheese sauce, cranberry salad and homemade biscuits," Mary said as she began placing the dishes of food on the table.

"I think I've gained about ten pounds since you started working for me," he replied. "You are definitely a great cook."

"Thank you. I've always enjoyed cooking," she replied. She sat and began to fill Annabelle's plate. "Agnes used to give me free rein in her kitchen and encouraged me to get creative with the cooking."

"Then thank goodness for Agnes. Have you spoken to her since she moved to Indiana?" he asked.

She smiled. "I just spoke to her last night, and she's very happy. She's actually moved in with her son and is enjoying spending time with grandbabies and great-grandbabies."

"That's nice."

"Daddy, look… I eat the green stuff." Annabelle took a bite of the cheesy broccoli and then grinned broadly.

"That's wonderful, honey. Green stuff is good for you," he replied. Love for his little girl swelled up in his heart. Was he shortchanging her by deciding to never marry again? Would she one day resent him for not providing a present and loving stepmother?

"How was your day?" Mary asked once the plates were all filled.

"I mostly worked in the barn today. I'm trying to get it cleaned up and organized—something I haven't done since last year. I'd like to have it done by fall. I'm also checking supplies and getting together another list of things to order."

"Sounds like a big job. Are the men who work for you helping with the barn cleanup?" she asked.

"No. That's a job I always do by myself," he replied.

"What kinds of things do you have to order?"

He knew she wasn't just asking the question to make conversation; Mary always seemed genuinely curious about farming. She wanted to learn new things and understand what he did during his day.

Funny—when he looked back in time, he realized Diana had rarely asked him about his day and never wanted to talk about his work. She found it all quite boring.

It was only a fleeting thought before he answered Mary's question. As they ate, the conversation moved on from ranching to her day with Annabelle.

"I've set up a playdate for tomorrow between one and three. Max and Jessica Patrick's little boy and Jim and Regina Sampson's little girl are coming over," she said.

"Playdate," Annabelle said, clapping her hands together. "Friends, Daddy."

"Yes, friends, bug," he replied.

"Daddy, I not a bug," she said and giggled.

He looked back at Mary. "Are you sure you're feeling up to a playdate?"

"I'm feeling just fine. The bruising is nearly gone, and all the aches and pains have gone away," she replied. She smiled—the smile that always shot a warmth deep into his belly. "I'm actually looking forward to the playdate. It should be lots of fun for Annabelle."

"Fun," Annabelle chimed in. "We have fun, Daddy."

They finished up dinner, and while she cleared the dishes, he went into the living room to spend time with his daughter. As usual, she wanted to play baby dolls, and Lucas found himself changing pretend diapers and feeding pretend chocolate cake to a baby. It was time that he treasured, knowing each day his baby girl was growing and changing.

In a perfect world, he would have liked more children. He would have liked to have at least two more— but his was not a perfect world. And it seemed to get more confusing by the day.

Being around Mary had become an exquisite form of torture, and yet night after night, he invited her to watch television with him. Night after night, he actively sought out her company.

Tonight was no different. When Annabelle was tucked into bed and sleeping, the two of them settled in to watch television.

He had just tuned in to one of their favorite shows when a knock sounded on the door. He paused the television and then went to see who was there.

"Hey, man, what are you doing here at this time of night?" Lucas asked Dallas.

"I'm here to check in with Mary," Dallas replied.

"Come on in. She's in the living room." Lucas led Dallas into the room, where Mary was seated on the sofa.

"Hi, Dallas." Mary started to stand, but he waved her back down.

"Hi, Mary. I just thought I'd come by and update you on the investigation and what we've been doing to find the pickup that crashed into you."

"Dallas, please sit," Lucas said and gestured to the side of the sofa opposite from Mary. Dallas nodded and took a seat, while Lucas returned to his recliner.

"How are you feeling, Mary?" Dallas asked.

"Completely back to normal," she replied.

"Well, I wish I had some good news to bring to you, but unfortunately, we have yet to find the pickup in question. We've checked all the garages in the general area to find one that had a pickup brought in for front-end damage. We've reached out as far as Kansas City and Topeka in an effort to find it, but we've come up empty-handed."

Lucas saw Mary deflate a bit. "I certainly appreciate all your hard work on my behalf," she said.

"I wish I could have come with better news," Dallas replied.

"So where do you think this truck is?" Lucas asked.

Dallas shrugged. "For all I know, it's parked in some shed or barn within a ten-mile radius from where we're sitting right now."

"Well, that's a frustrating thought," Lucas said.

"Lately everything is frustrating to me." Dallas sighed deeply. "I also checked out the Farmer's Club and Murphy's to see if anyone who'd had too much to drink left their bars that night around the same time. We came up empty-handed there, too." He stood. "Once again, I'm sorry I didn't bring any good news with me."

"Thank you for stopping by, Dallas," Mary said. "I understand you can only do so much."

"Yeah, well, I wish I could have done more," the lawman replied. "We're going to keep at it, Mary."

"I'll walk you out," Lucas said.

The two men stepped out into the early evening. "To be honest, I don't think I'm going to find that pickup," Dallas said. "And I'm leaning toward believing it was a drunk driver who not only ran from the scene but then sobered up and realized he or she struck somebody. Now they're hiding the pickup and waiting until the heat is off."

"So you don't think it was a deliberate act?" Lucas asked.

"I can't be one hundred percent positive, but I keep thinking about the fact that Mary said the truck was weaving all over the road before it struck her. That, to me, sounds more like a drunk driver than a deliberate act," Dallas said as they walked toward his car in the driveway.

"Then I'll tell Mary that. I'm sure it will make her feel a little better about what happened. It sure as hell makes me feel better."

"Like I said, I can't be absolutely sure about it, but the facts lend themselves toward a drunk driver."

Dallas opened his car door. "Now, if I could just get a break on Cindy Perry's murder."

"Still nothing?" Lucas asked.

"Absolutely nothing," Dallas replied and then released a deep sigh. "When I do find the bastard who killed her, then you and I are going to take an evening and grab a few beers together."

"That sounds good to me. It's been too long since we did that."

The two said their goodbyes, and as Dallas drove down the driveway, Lucas turned to go back into the house—back to Mary, the woman who filled his dreams at night, the woman who tormented him with her scent...with her beautiful smiles...with her very presence.

As a warm evening breeze flowed over him, he stood on the front porch and tried to evoke a picture of Diana in his head. It scared him just a little bit when the only picture he got in his mind was Mary's face, with her long, shiny brown hair and her vivid green eyes.

It scared him even more when he couldn't remember the sound of Diana's laughter, but Mary's musical laughter came easily to his mind.

What was happening to him? He felt as if he was losing his mind. He stepped into the house but stopped at the accent table in the hallway. He pulled open the drawer and withdrew the photo Nicole had brought to him.

There she was: the dark-haired, blue-eyed woman

he would love forever. He stared at her for several long minutes, drinking his fill of her until he felt strong enough to go back into the living room and spend time with Mary.

The playdate was in full swing in Annabelle's room. Mary sat in a chair in the corner and watched the children interact with each other. They were one hour into it, and it was easy to pick out characteristics of the two new kids.

Cute little Bobby Patrick had thick brown hair and brown eyes. He was the shyest of the three. Then there was Jill Sampson. She was red-haired and freckled and had the same outgoing energy as Annabelle. The three had instantly become best friends.

"How about we go in the kitchen and get a snack?" Practically before the words were out of Mary's mouth, the children cheered and raced for the kitchen.

Since Mary didn't have three booster seats, she sat the kids in a circle on the floor. Earlier that morning, she had prepared celery sticks slathered with peanut butter, and apple slices with a caramel dip. She had also baked cupcakes that morning.

She'd planned on giving them cookies, but unfortunately, there were no cookies left in the house. After giving them each a small carton of milk, Mary then sat at the table.

She had promised Annabelle cookies before bedtime if she behaved well during the playdate. So far, Annabelle had been a wonderful little hostess. She'd easily shared all her toys, and when Bobby got quiet and shy, she'd encouraged him to play with her.

"Come on, Bobby," she'd say and throw an arm around his neck. "We friends. Play with me and Jill."

So far, Mary owed Annabelle her favorite cookies before bedtime, and that meant she would need to drive into town right after dinner.

The children were gone at exactly three, and Mary immediately put Annabelle down for a late nap. Once she was sleeping, Mary hurried back to the kitchen to begin dinner.

As always, when she had a minute to think, her thoughts went to Lucas. For the past couple of nights, things had been strange between them.

He'd become quiet and distant, only answering questions when she asked them. Was he growing unhappy with her? She supposed if worse came to worst, she could move into the Millsville Motel until she found another place to live and a job that would pay for it.

Her heart absolutely clenched at the thought of not being here, of not being part of their lives. At least he'd paid her well enough that she had a small nest egg saved up. She'd hoped to use it for school in the fall, but if he fired her, she'd need it to pay for a place to live.

Maybe she was just too deep in her head. He hadn't specifically said anything about being unhappy with her. Maybe it was just time for her to start spending some evenings in her room and giving him some space.

By the time he came in the back door for dinner, Mary had put all her negative thoughts out of her mind. She and Annabelle greeted him with smiles.

"Daddy, I got friends," Annabelle said.

"You do? What are your friends' names?" he asked.

"Bobby and Jill. I like them, Daddy. I like them a lot, and they are my new friends. I let them play with all my toys. Right, Ms. Mary?"

"Right. I was very proud of you, Annabelle. Your daddy would have been proud of you, too," Mary said, smiling at the little girl.

"And I get cookies before the sleep fairies come tonight. Right, Ms. Mary? I get the cookies with the stripes, right?"

"Right," Mary said to Annabelle and then turned her attention to Lucas. "I promised her if she was a good hostess, then she could have her favorite cookies before bedtime," Mary explained. "Of course, that's only if it's okay with you."

"Sounds good to me. I might have a couple of cookies with you, Annabelle." He grinned at his daughter and then grinned at Mary. "And now I'm going to jump in the shower really quick before dinner." With that, he left the kitchen.

Twenty minutes later, he was back, smelling like minty soap and the cologne he wore. The scent always stirred a touch of warmth through her body. It brought up memories of the night they had made love.

Tonight, the conversation as they ate revolved around the playdate. Annabelle was an active participant in the talk, telling her daddy everything she had done with her new friends.

When dinner was over, Lucas and Annabelle went into the living room while Mary cleared the dishes. Once she cleaned the kitchen, she went to her bedroom to grab her purse.

She headed back into the living room, where Lucas and Annabelle were building towers with the big blocks. "I need to make a quick run to the grocery store," she said. "Is there anything you need or want while I'm there?"

"I can't think of anything," he said. "Wouldn't you rather wait until morning to go?"

"I can't," she replied. "I'm out of the promised treat."

"Ah. I'm sure she would understand if you had to put it off until tomorrow night," he replied.

"Look, Ms. Mary. Daddy made a tower," Annabelle said. She jumped up and down and then crashed into it and giggled as the blocks fell to the floor.

"Oh, no!" Lucas replied with pretend sadness. "Somebody knocked down my tower."

"Daddy, it was me. I did it," Annabelle said and then giggled once again.

"Looks like you need to build another tower,"

Mary said with a laugh. "And a promise is a promise, so I'll be back in about forty minutes or so."

"Drive carefully, and we'll see you when you get home," Lucas replied.

"See you, Ms. Mary," Annabelle chimed in.

Minutes later, Mary was in her rental car, headed toward town.

She'd felt a lot better about things since Dallas had told Lucas he really believed her accident had been due to a drunk driver. Still, whenever she drove, she kept a close eye on her rearview mirror to make sure nobody crept up on her.

She had her eye on a cute little compact car in the used-car lot. She planned to buy it as soon as she received a check from the insurance company, which was supposed to be in the works. It would be nice to be back in a car she could call her very own.

It was a beautiful evening. Although warm, the sky was a gorgeous blue. Wispy white clouds chased each other, and a light breeze blew from the south.

Instead of running the air conditioner, she opened her window. The smells that greeted her were of sun-baked earth and healthy crops, and suddenly she was back in that place where she'd smelled these same scents and had found a human scarecrow.

A vision of Cindy filled her head. The horrifying memory nearly stole her breath away. It had been so horrific and terrifying. She wished Cindy's killer was behind bars…or rotting someplace in hell.

Thankfully, at least nobody else had been turned

into a scarecrow. Mary just wished she knew what had been going on in Cindy's private life that might have prompted somebody to do that to her.

Mary rolled her window back up and turned on the air conditioner, hoping that might chase the memory away. All she wanted to do was get to the grocery store, grab the promised package of cookies and then get back home.

The playdate had been a rousing success, but she had to admit that chasing after three little ones had worn her out. She was more tired tonight than usual.

When she pulled up at the grocery store, she breathed a sigh of relief. There were only a few cars parked in front, which meant she should be able to get in and out in no time.

The first person she saw inside was Celeste Winthrop. The beautiful blonde gave her a cold glare and then turned her back to proceed up an aisle without speaking a word to her.

That woman is definitely rude, Mary thought as she hurried to the cookie aisle. Once there, she grabbed a package of Annabelle's favorite cookies and then hurried on to the checkout.

Sally was working, and what should have been a minutes-long checkout went way longer, as Sally visited with her and nobody stepped up in line behind Mary.

After about fifteen minutes of chitchat, Mary finally said she needed to go. "Sally, I really need to get these cookies home to Annabelle before her bedtime."

"Of course," Sally said and rang her up. "I wouldn't want to be the reason that cute little girl missed out on her cookies before bedtime." Mary paid, said good-bye and then left the store. She had nearly reached her car when somebody called out to her.

She walked over to the other car. "Hi," she said in surprise.

"Mary, I think we need to talk. Why don't you get in and chat with me for a couple of minutes?"

Mary frowned, wondering what on earth they needed to discuss. "Okay," she finally said. "But I can't take too long. I have cookies for Annabelle."

Mary opened her passenger door and set the cookies on her passenger seat. She then walked around the other car and slid into that passenger seat. "What's up?" she asked curiously.

The other woman leaned over and grabbed hold of Mary's arm. Mary felt a sharp jab in her shoulder and jumped back. She looked down to see a hypodermic needle hanging from her blouse. "Wh-what have you done?" she asked breathlessly. As she stared at the other woman, her vision began to blur. "Why…why? What have you done?" Her voice became slurred, and she struggled to get out of the car, but she felt like she was moving in slow motion.

She fumbled with the car-door handle, but she couldn't make it work. What was happening? Oh, God, what was happening? She was in trouble. She was in deep trouble. This was her last conscious thought before darkness descended and swallowed her up whole.

Chapter 11

Lucas looked at his watch with a frown. Mary had been gone a little over an hour now, and a sliver of worry whispered inside him. He tried to dismiss it as being ridiculous. After all, he knew it would probably take her forty to forty-five minutes or so to drive into town, buy the cookies and then get back home.

There could be a lot of reasons why it was taking her a little longer. The main one would be that she had lots of friends and former coworkers in the grocery store who might want to visit with her.

There was no reason to worry about her—except suddenly, he was thinking about the note she'd received and the fact that somebody had crashed into her car hard enough to make her spin out of control and roll over and over again.

"Annabelle, it's time to put your toys away and get into the bathtub," he said to his daughter.

"Five more minutes, 'kay, Daddy? Five more minutes to play, 'kay?" She gave him a charming smile.

"Okay, five more minutes," he agreed. It was just a little after six, and the sun was still shining bright. Mary would probably be arriving back home any moment now.

When five minutes had passed, he helped Annabelle put all the toys away, and then got her into a bathtub full of strawberry-scented bubbles. He was aware of each minute ticking away. Where on earth was Mary?

By the time he got Annabelle out of the tub and into her pajamas, a full-on alarm had begun screeching in his head. He tried to tell himself that Mary was off duty, that she didn't owe him a certain time to be home.

But he knew that Mary was nothing if not conscious of her promises to Annabelle, and she would never dally around when she'd promised the little girl cookies before bedtime.

"You can go ahead and play in your room for a little while," he told his daughter. "Daddy has to make some phone calls."

"'Kay," Annabelle replied and headed to her bedroom.

He immediately called Mary's phone. It went straight to voice mail. So it was either dead or she'd turned it off. The fact that he couldn't reach her only increased the alarm that was racing through him.

It was now after six thirty, and she had left around five o'clock. He reminded himself again that she didn't have a curfew, and she certainly didn't owe him her time when she was off duty. She didn't even owe it to him to check in with him. Maybe she'd had other errands to run. Still, she'd said it would be a fast trip for cookies and nothing more.

At seven, he finally broke down and called Dallas. "Hey, I hate to bother you, and I might be overreacting, but I'm worried about Mary," he said.

"Worried how?" Dallas asked.

"She left here at just after five to run into town and buy some cookies, but she isn't home yet. She didn't mention any other errands and, in fact, specifically said she'd be back in forty minutes or so. Two hours have passed, and she still isn't home."

"Have you tried to call her?" Dallas asked.

"Yes, several times, and the calls go straight to voice mail."

"Is she still driving that blue rental car?"

"Yes, she is," Lucas replied.

"I'll drive by the grocery store and see what I can find out. Maybe that rental had problems and she's stuck somewhere with a dead cell phone on the side of the road."

"Call me as soon as you find her, okay?" Lucas asked.

"Absolutely," Dallas replied. "I'll talk to you later."

Lucas felt a little better knowing Dallas was out actively looking for her. Lucas hadn't thought about car trouble. Maybe that was what had happened. Nothing nefarious…just car issues. The rental car wasn't new, so it was quite possible it'd had some kind of engine trouble.

He sank down in his recliner with his cell phone in his hand. Hopefully, Dallas would call back quickly and let him know Mary was safe and sound.

"Daddy, I get cookies?" Annabelle asked as she came into the living room.

"Just as soon as Ms. Mary gets home," he replied. "Why don't you get up here on the sofa to wait for her?" He knew the odds of getting her to bed right now were against him. But it was her bedtime, and with a yawn, she got up on the sofa.

Within minutes, Annabelle was sound asleep. Lucas got a blanket from her bedroom and covered her up. He then sat back down and waited for Dallas to call.

It didn't take long before Dallas was on the phone. "Her car is parked in front of the grocery store, but she isn't here."

For a moment, Dallas's words didn't compute.

"What do you mean, she's not there? If the car is there, then she has to be someplace around."

"Sally said she checked Mary out well over an hour and a half ago, and Mary said she was headed straight back home. She's no place in the grocery store. I'm going to grab some men and have them check the stores along Main Street to see if she's in one of them."

"So basically what you're telling me right now is that Mary is missing." The alarm bells that had been ringing softly in Lucas's head now clanged discordantly as a very real fear rushed through him.

"Yeah, right now, that's what I'm telling you," Dallas said tersely.

"As soon as I find somebody to stay here with Annabelle, I'll be there to help the search for her." Lucas didn't wait for a reply. He immediately hung up and dialed Nicole.

She answered on the third ring. "Nicole, I was wondering if you could come over and watch Annabelle."

"Oh… I… Where's Mary?" Nicole's voice sounded weak and half-breathless.

"That's the thing… She's missing."

"*Missing?* What on earth do you mean?"

Lucas quickly explained the situation to her. "I was wondering if you could come over and watch Annabelle so I could go into town to help search for her, but you don't sound very well."

"Yes, I'm having a really bad night. I'm already in bed, but if you need me…"

"No. No, you stay in bed," Lucas said. "I'll try to get Ramona over here. I'll just talk to you later."

"Please let me know what's going on when you find out," Nicole said.

"I'll call you as soon as I know something." Lucas disconnected from Nicole and immediately punched in the number for Ramona.

Ramona Benjamin was a twenty-two-year-old who occasionally babysat for Lucas when Nicole wasn't available. She had always been dependable and responsible. Lucas only hoped she would be available on such short notice.

Thankfully, she was free, and she promised to be over within twenty minutes. While he waited for her, he moved Annabelle from the sofa to her bed. He was glad she didn't wake up from the move.

He'd hoped Dallas would have called back with the news that he'd found Mary and she was okay, but Lucas's phone remained silent. That silence pressed heavy and tight against his chest.

What could have happened to her? Where could she have gone without her car? Lucas's fear grew bigger and bigger with each minute that passed.

Finally, Ramona arrived. He explained to her that he had no idea how late he might be, and she assured him she had all night long to help him out.

When he got in his truck, his muscles were tense

and his heart was beating in the unnatural rhythm of fear. They had to find her. They just had to.

He drove as fast as possible, eager to get to town and start looking for her. Maybe she went into another store and passed out in an aisle and nobody had found her yet. Maybe she somehow hit her head and was now wandering around town with a form of amnesia.

God, he was grasping at straws, and he knew it. Or maybe somebody had grabbed her—the same somebody who had left the note... The same somebody who had tried to kill her by crashing into her car. That was his most horrifying thought.

He gripped the steering wheel tightly, his heart beating a million beats a minute. If she had been taken, then who was responsible?

Had she gotten into somebody else's car? Who would she trust enough to do that? Celeste? Gina? Those were the only names that popped into his head. But did he really believe they could be responsible for this? Would she really trust either one of them enough to get into their car?

He finally reached the grocery store, where Dallas's cop car sat next to Mary's rental. As Lucas parked and got out of his truck, he saw Dallas and several of his officers approaching him from down the sidewalk. Lucas hurried over to meet them.

"Anything?" Lucas asked.

Dallas shook his head. "Nothing. My men and I

have canvassed the area, and as far as we know, nobody other than Sally saw Mary this evening."

"I'm going in to talk to Sally. Maybe she saw something or somebody who was in the store at the same time as Mary." Lucas didn't wait for a response. He turned around and headed into the store. He was aware of Dallas at his heels as he approached Sally.

Luckily, there was nobody in her line, and she greeted Lucas with a worried frown. "Are you all still looking for Mary?" she asked.

"We are," Lucas said, his chest tightening painfully. "Sally, did she mention anything at all about having other errands to run?"

"No. In fact, she cut our visiting short, telling me she needed to get those cookies home before Annabelle's bedtime," Sally said. "Dallas already talked to me, and I told him the same thing."

"The cookies are in her car," Dallas said.

So she'd made it from the store to her car. *What happened to her then?* Lucas wondered. "Who was in the store at the same time as Mary?" he asked.

Sally shrugged. "Not that many people." She frowned thoughtfully. "That nasty Fred Stanley came in, bought a quart of ice cream and then asked me if I wanted to perform a sex act on him. He's such a nasty old man."

She paused a moment and then continued. "Ethan Dourty also came in around that time. He bought two steaks and a bottle of wine. Gloria Young was in here and checked out right after Mary left the store. Oh, and Celeste Winthrop was also in here. She bought the fixings to make an apple pie. Awfully early in the season for that, and she bought premade piecrusts. And I think that's everyone who was in here around the time Mary was."

Lucas didn't give a damn what those people had bought, but two names definitely caught his attention. Mary had indicated earlier that Ethan Dourty always wanted to dance with her whenever they were both at Murphy's. And then there was Celeste, who he knew had been cold and rude to Mary in the past—a woman who might want Mary out of his house and out of her way.

He grabbed Dallas's arm and propelled him back out the entrance door. "We need to check out Ethan and Celeste," he said urgently. "I think it's possible one of them might have an obsession with Mary." He quickly explained how Ethan was always dancing with Mary at Murphy's and how Celeste had shown she had a jealous streak on more than one occasion.

"I find Ethan to be a bit of a stretch," Dallas replied. "Just because he dances with Mary at Murphy's doesn't mean he's obsessed with her. But we can definitely head to Celeste's home and see what's going on there."

"I'll be right behind you," Lucas said.

"You know the best thing you could do right now is go home and stay home in case she calls you.

Leave the rest of this up to me and my men," Dallas replied.

"The only phone I have is my cell phone, and I'm not about to sit home twiddling my thumbs while she's missing." Lucas held Dallas's gaze intently. "I need to be a part of this, Dallas. Please."

Dallas hesitated a moment and then gave a curt nod. "Okay, then. Let's go check out Celeste."

Minutes later, Lucas was following Dallas's car. Twilight had fallen, portending the darkness of the night to come. He wanted her home before dark. God, he needed her safe at home right now.

His chest was so tight with anxiety he felt like he could barely draw his next breath. *Mary... Mary, where are you?* his heart cried out. *Annabelle needs you... I need you.*

Celeste lived in a two-story house on a quiet tree-lined street. Dallas pulled into her driveway, and Lucas parked at the curb. Together they headed to the front door.

Celeste answered on the second knock. She was wrapped in a blue robe, and her eyes opened wide at the sight of them. "Celeste, can we come in?" Dallas asked. "We need to speak to you."

"Of course." She opened the door wider to allow them entry. She gestured toward the sofa, but the two men remained standing. She picked up a remote and lowered the sound on the television. "What do you need to speak to me about?"

"Celeste, when was the last time you saw Mary Curtis?" Dallas asked.

"Mary? I saw her briefly in the grocery store earlier this evening. Why?" She looked at Dallas, then Lucas and then back again at Dallas. "Dallas, what's going on?"

Lucas knew Mary wasn't here. He knew it in his gut. Celeste looked genuinely confused, and there was absolutely no indication she'd done anything to Mary. There was no sound, no smell, hinting that Mary was or had been here.

Dallas explained what had happened to Celeste. "So do you mind if we take a quick look around?"

"Of course not, but I find it a little offensive that you would think I had anything to do with whatever happened to her," she said coolly.

"I'm sorry if you're offended, Celeste, but I'm just doing my job," Dallas replied.

Lucas said nothing. He didn't care if Celeste was a little offended or highly offended. All he wanted was to find Mary. It took them ten long minutes to check out all the rooms in the house, including the basement.

"Thank you, Celeste," Dallas said when they were finished.

"I hope you find her," Celeste replied. "I'll admit, I've been rather rude to her in the past, but I've never wished any kind of harm on her."

They left Celeste's place and then headed for Ethan Dourty's house. With each moment that passed, the urgency Lucas felt inside grew more overwhelming. What had happened to her?

Darkness had fallen, bringing with it a sense of helplessness...of hopelessness. Dear God, where was Mary?

Mary slowly came to. Her head filled with the scent of hay and dust and other smells she didn't recognize. She fought to open her eyes. She was still so sleepy...so groggy. Why was she sleeping? She needed to wake up and take care of Annabelle. It had to be morning since she'd been sleeping.

She tried to move her arms. She couldn't. Why couldn't she move? She tried to adjust her legs with the same result.

Panic caused her eyes to snap open, and she looked around wildly. Now she saw why she couldn't move— she was tied to a wooden chair. Thick ropes not only bound her arms and legs, but another one was also wrapped tightly around her upper chest.

The chair was in what appeared to be an old barn. On one side of the barn, a vehicle was parked and covered with tarps. There was a workbench nearby, and on top of it, she saw a flannel shirt, a pair of jeans...and a straw hat. Immediately, Mary was shot back in time.

Blue skies...the scent of cornstalks filling the air...and then horror. Cindy on a stake, her eyes missing and her mouth sewn shut.

Mary closed her eyes. Was she dreaming? Was

this some sort of nightmare? She opened her eyes again. No, this was real. This was all horrifyingly real.

Once again, she thought of Cindy, and she stared at the items on the workbench. Oh, God, was that about to happen to her? Did the person who had killed Cindy now intend to make Mary a human scarecrow? No…no, that wasn't right. It wasn't some crazed madman who had drugged her and tied her up.

It all now slammed back into her head, memories of the moments before she fell sleep. She'd gotten the cookies for Annabelle and then walked out of the store. She now remembered the car that had been parked next to hers. She'd had no fear when she slid into the passenger seat. And then the jab in the shoulder…and darkness.

She tried to fight against the ropes. She worked her wrists, pulling and tugging. But the ropes held tight. Her breaths came out in frantic pants as she tried desperately to get free.

Panic swelled up inside her, and her struggles increased. She fought the ropes until her wrists felt raw and she was breathless from the panicked gasps that escaped her. Tears of frustration welled up and coursed down her cheeks as she realized she was tied so tightly she couldn't get free.

She began to scream as loud as she could. "Somebody, help me!" she yelled over and over again, until she had no breath left.

For the next several minutes, she sobbed. Tears ran hot down her cheeks. She was in deep trouble. Nobody knew what had happened to her. Nobody knew where she was.

She finally swallowed against her tears, pulled herself together and began to wrestle with the ropes once again. She had to get free. Somehow…someway, she had to get away.

The door to the barn creaked open, and her captor walked in. She stared at her in disbelief. "What's going on? What are you doing?"

The beautiful dark-haired woman smiled at her. "I'm getting rid of you, Mary. You didn't pay attention to the note I left for you, and you miraculously crawled out of the wreckage of your car."

Mary was momentarily stunned. "You left the note for me? You were the one who crashed into my car and made me wreck? Why? Why are you doing this to me?"

Nicole's eyes narrowed, and her upper lip lifted in a snarl. "Because I see how he looks at you. You're making him forget my daughter. He's in love with you, and that's not acceptable. That's not acceptable at all. He promised to love Diana forever, and you're making him forget. You have to be gone. It's the only way to fix things."

"Nicole, please untie me and let me go." Despite the screams Mary wanted to release, she attempted to speak calmly to the woman, hoping she could get through to her. "You are mistaken about things.

Lucas isn't in love with me. I'm just the housekeeper and nanny for him."

"Maybe right now, but he looks at you like he used to look at Diana," Nicole replied. "He's in love with you, and you have to go." Her anger simmered just beneath the surface, but Mary felt it wafting toward her. It felt evil. It felt sick.

"Nicole, just let me go. I'll…I'll stop working for him. I'll move far away from here, and I won't tell anyone what's happened." The words tumbled from Mary's mouth. She was frantic to get through to the older woman. She was desperate to make this all end now.

"Shut up," Nicole snapped. "I don't believe you. Besides, it's a perfect opportunity to get rid of you permanently. All I have to do is finish the preparations."

"Wh-what preparations?" Mary asked. Her heart beat so quickly she could scarcely catch her breath. She wanted to scream and cry, but she tried to keep her emotions under control. She hoped she could talk Nicole out of whatever she had planned. "Nicole, what preparations?" she repeated.

"You're going to be the next human scarecrow," Nicole replied with a sick glee in her voice.

Even though Mary had known that someplace in the back of her mind, hearing it spoken aloud shot icy horror through her. "D-did you do that to Cindy?"

"Heavens, no. I have no idea who killed Cindy.

But this is a perfect opportunity to take advantage of that murder. I'll kill you and make you a scarecrow, and Dallas will spin his wheels looking for a serial killer."

"You'll never get it right," Mary replied fervently. "You don't know exactly what was done to Cindy. You don't know all the details. Dallas will know it's a copycat killer."

"Nonsense. I know enough. Now, shut up so I can finish things up. I need to cut the bottom of these jeans so they look like scarecrow pants."

"How do you think you're going to get those jeans on me?" Mary asked.

Nicole grinned at her. "The same way I got you out of my car and into that chair. Once you're dead, I'll get you dressed and on a stake." She turned toward the workbench. "Oh, at least you'll be planted beneath a full moon tonight. That's always good luck."

"Nicole…please, you don't have to do this," Mary cried. "Please, let me go. This isn't the way to deal with your grief over Diana."

Nicole whirled around, her eyes once again blazing with rage. "Shut up. Don't you even mention her name. You aren't good enough to speak her name. Now, if you don't shut your mouth, I'll drug you again, and you will never, ever wake up. Is that what you want?"

"No," Mary replied. If she was drugged, then there would be no hope for her at all. If she was drugged, then she wouldn't have these last few minutes to think about Lucas and the love she had for him.

She wanted to take this time to remember the sound of his deep laughter, the magic of making love with him. She needed to take these final moments and lock her memories of him and Annabelle deep in her heart.

And somehow, someway, she hoped Dallas or somebody would find her before she was killed and trussed up like a scarecrow.

Chapter 12

"Where do we go next?" Dallas asked Lucas as they left Ethan Dourty's house.

Lucas's head spun. He was so frightened for Mary he could hardly think. Where could she be? Who had taken her away from him? "Gina Hightower." The name popped into his head. "It's possible Gina did something to Mary in a fit of jealousy. Gina has made it very clear she wants to be my next wife, and she might see Mary as standing in her way."

"Then let's go check her out," Dallas replied.

Once again, Lucas was in his truck, following Dallas's vehicle. His heart banged painfully in his chest. So much time had passed since Mary had gone missing. The minutes had turned into hours, and still she hadn't been found.

Were they already too late? Had something tragic, something horrible, already happened to her? Oh, God, he couldn't think that way. If he let that thought sink in and take hold, he'd be too devastated to even function.

If Gina didn't have Mary, then he had no idea where else to look. What else could have happened to her? Somebody had to have taken Mary from the grocery store—but who?

He had to hope that Gina had her and that no harm had come to her yet. He had to believe there was still time to find her…to *save* her. All he knew, in the very depths of his heart, was that she was in trouble—terrible trouble.

Gina lived in a small farmhouse on the edge of town. It was a charming, neat-looking place, with only a shed as an outbuilding. When they pulled into the driveway, the front porch light came on.

As Dallas and Lucas got out of their vehicles and approached the house, Gina stepped outside on the porch. "Dallas? Lucas? What's going on?" she asked.

"Gina, when was the last time you saw Mary Curtis?" Dallas asked.

"Mary?" She frowned. "I don't know. I think the last time I saw her was with you, Lucas. When I came over to pick up my pot. Why?"

"She's missing," Dallas said curtly. He was obviously feeling the same pressure as Lucas.

"*Missing?* What do you mean?"

"She was at the grocery store to pick up some

cookies. Her car is still parked there, but we can't find her," Dallas explained.

"It's been hours," Lucas added.

"And that's why you're here? You think I might have her tied up in my kitchen? Stowed away in my shed?" she asked incredulously. She looked at Lucas. "My God, Lucas, I told you I'd be better for you than her, but that doesn't mean I'd hurt her."

She opened the door and stepped to the side. "Please, feel free to come in and look around. I can't believe the two of you think I might have anything to do with this."

"We're checking out everyone who has had contact with Mary and Lucas," Dallas said. "We'll be out of here in just a few minutes."

Once again, they checked room after room and found no evidence that Mary was or had ever been present in the house. They even checked out the shed, which held only tools and a lawn mower. An overwhelming sense of helplessness crept through Lucas.

"Anyone else to check out?" Dallas asked as they stepped outside Gina's place.

"Dallas, I don't know where to go from here," Lucas admitted helplessly. His heart felt heavy in his chest.

"Why don't we meet back in my office for some brainstorming, and I'll call in more men to join the search."

Lucas nodded. He felt sick. He'd never believed he would feel this kind of raw grief for a second time in his life. But that was what he was feeling, the grief over losing Mary.

As he drove back into town, the same questions rolled over and over in his mind. Where was she? Who had her? Who…? *Who?* He racked his brain. They'd checked off the people whom he'd thought could be potential suspects. He had no idea what direction to go next, and that scared him as much as anything.

What if it was nobody on their radar? If Mary got into somebody's car, she would have known them. But what if she'd been physically bullied into a waiting car? What if somebody had knocked her unconscious and then had put her into their car? Who would do that? Who had Mary? And was she being held somewhere? Where?

Dammit, why had there been nobody on the street or in the area to see what had happened to her? Why had fate put her in danger with no witnesses to help them find her?

The questions continued to spin around and around in his mind, making him feel ridiculous as he tried to think of answers. Hot tears burned in his eyes, but he swallowed hard against them. He wasn't going to allow himself to weep yet. He needed to stay strong for Mary.

When they arrived at the police station, instead of Dallas leading him into his private office, he took him to a small conference room. Dallas gestured toward a seat at the long table, and then he walked over to the whiteboard that hung on one wall.

"As we drove back here, I called in five more men. I also called everyone on duty now and told them to check in here. We need to have a coordinated search going on," Dallas said. "You know I don't have a large force at my disposal, so we need to work smart. You keep thinking about anyone who might have an issue with Mary."

"What about that Kenny guy who was sending her those nasty emails and texts?"

"I already checked him out. The first thing I did when we discovered Mary missing was reach out to the St. Louis Police Department. They made contact with Kenny, who was at his house. There's no way he would have had time to come here, grab Mary and then get back to St. Louis."

"So it's got to be somebody here in town," Lucas replied. He slammed his fists down on the table, anger and fear exploding from him. "Dammit, who? Who has done this? She was the sweetest woman in the world. She didn't have any enemies."

He stopped, appalled as he recognized all of a sudden that he was speaking about her in the past tense, as if it was already too late… As if she was already dead.

"We've got to find her, Dallas," he finally said in desperation. "She has to be someplace close by."

"I'm trying, Lucas. There was no sign of a struggle around her car. We know it's possible she got into another vehicle. Who would she trust enough to do that?"

"I don't know," Lucas replied. "I can't think of anyone she'd trust enough to get into their car." He frowned thoughtfully. "Maybe Nicole, but I talked to her earlier. She said she was having a bad night and was in bed."

"Did you believe her?"

The question caught Lucas by surprise. "I had no reason not to believe her. Why would you ask that?"

"Lucas, I've known you for years. I know how much you loved Diana, and I know how much you've grieved her passing. But you have a new light in your eyes and a warmth in your voice when you mention Mary's name. If *I* see it and hear it, maybe it's possible Nicole has seen it and heard it as well. Maybe she is threatened by it. Maybe she sees Mary as a threat to her daughter's memory."

"But that's absurd," Lucas replied. "I will never forget Diana or the memories I have of her. She has a part of my heart that will never go away. Hell, she was the mother of my daughter."

"I know that," Dallas replied. He shrugged. "It was just a passing thought."

At that moment, two patrolmen came in. As Dallas spoke to them, Lucas kept working what his friend had said about Nicole around in his head.

Was it really possible? Nicole had always been friendly to Mary. Still, there was no question Nicole worked hard to keep Diana alive in Lucas's life. Was it really possible that somehow Nicole had gotten Mary in her car and taken her away somewhere? Mary certainly would have been willing to get into Nicole's car. Nicole was big enough, strong enough, to overpower Mary.

"Dallas, we need to check out Nicole's place," Lucas said urgently. He got up from the table. He had no idea if Nicole might be behind Mary's disappearance, but he couldn't leave any stone unturned in looking for her.

"You can follow us," Dallas said to Pete and Tim, the other two patrolmen. "Let's go."

Minutes later, Lucas was once again in his truck, following Dallas's vehicle and the other patrol car with the two officers. Was this just a wild-goose chase? Were they just wasting more time—precious time—when they could be searching elsewhere?

It was hard for him to believe his mother-in-law would do anything to harm Mary—to harm *anyone*— but at the moment, he didn't know what to think. All he really knew was he wanted Mary home safe and sound.

Was Nicole really having a bad night, or had she been busy doing something to Mary?

Nicole's place was at the very edge of town, and when they pulled up, the house was dark. An old barn and an old shed were visible in the shimmery light from the full moon overhead.

It appeared that Nicole was probably sound asleep. *Dammit.* Lucas knew this was probably just a wild-goose chase. Still, he followed Dallas, Pete and Tim up to the front door.

Dallas knocked on the door. They waited, but nobody came. Dallas knocked again, harder this time. Again, they waited, but there was no response from inside the house.

This time, Dallas banged on the door with enough force to wake the dead. "Nicole!" he yelled. "Nicole, it's Dallas. Come to the door."

Even if Nicole was sound asleep when they'd arrived, she should be awake now. Still, she didn't make an appearance. She was either dead or she wasn't home. Yet her car was parked in the drive.

In frustration, Lucas turned his back on the door and stared out at the barn. To Lucas's surprise, after Dallas yelled her name again, the barn door opened and Nicole stepped out, closing the door behind her.

"Dallas… Lucas… What's going on?" she asked as she approached them.

She looked disheveled, wearing an old pair of jeans and a black blouse. "I thought you'd gone to bed early because you were having a bad night," Lucas said.

"I did earlier, but I got to feeling better and decided to do a little work in the barn," she replied. "Why? Why are you all here?"

"Mary is still missing," Lucas said, laser focused on the woman who had been in his life for years.

"Oh, I'm sorry to hear that. But that doesn't explain why you're here. Surely you don't think I had anything to do with whatever happened to her," Nicole replied with a small laugh.

Lucas wasn't laughing. There was a strange light in Nicole's eyes—a light that suddenly made his skin crawl. "What kind of work are you doing in the barn?" he asked.

"Oh, just organizing some of the old tools and things," she replied, glancing back at the barn door.

"Strange time of night to be working in your barn," Dallas said.

She looked back at him. "It's the best time to be working out here. It's so much cooler at this time of night than trying to work in the heat of the day."

"Why don't you let me see what kind of work you're doing? Maybe I could come over and help you sometime," Lucas said.

"Oh, I don't want you to see it tonight. I've kind of made a mess of things in there. Come back tomorrow, and I'll show you in the daylight," Nicole replied. She stepped from one foot to the other, her gaze shooting from Lucas to Dallas and then back to Lucas. "I suggest you all go on and keep looking for Mary, because she certainly isn't here."

She threw a glance over her shoulder toward the barn and then gazed back at Lucas. "I'm sorry I can't help you. I have no idea where she might be."

"I'd still like to see the work you're doing in your barn. I promise I'll just take a quick peek." Lucas's heart beat with urgency as he headed toward the barn.

"No, I don't want you to see in there," Nicole said frantically.

Lucas kept walking. He gasped as Nicole jumped on his back, the unexpected weight of her nearly causing him to tumble to the ground. "I said not tonight!" she screamed.

"Whoa... Nicole, stop." Dallas jumped forward and grabbed her. Once he had control of her, Lucas ran for the barn. He was afraid—so afraid—that Nicole had done something to hurt Mary. He was almost too afraid to open the barn door, and yet he needed to get inside as soon as possible.

He finally reached the door and threw it open. Immediately, he saw Mary tied to a chair, her head down. As if it was already too late.

"Mary... Oh, God, Mary!" he cried, racing over to her. She raised her head. Her mouth was taped closed, and tears streaked down her cheeks. "Get me something to cut her loose," he said to the others, who had followed him inside.

"Let her die," Nicole yelled as she struggled against the tight hold Dallas had on her. "She was making you forget Diana. Don't you understand? Lucas, she has to die so my daughter can live on."

Lucas ignored Nicole as one of the officers handed him a knife from the worktable. The first thing he did was gently rip off the tape from Mary's mouth. She gasped, her face unnaturally pale. "She stabbed me, Lucas. She w-wanted to stab me to d-death."

It was then that Lucas saw the blood seeping out

from a wound just under her breast. "Somebody call for an ambulance!" Lucas exclaimed as he frantically worked to cut the ropes that bound her.

Mary continued to cry and moan while Nicole continued to rant and scream her madness. "Lucas, surely you understand. Mary is a threat. She's a threat to Diana. You are in love with Mary, and you promised to love only Diana."

"An ambulance is on its way," Tim said.

"Sh-she was g-going to make me a human sc-scarecrow," Mary said through her tears. "Sh-she was going to c-copycat so D-Dallas would think the s-same person who killed Cindy killed me."

Lucas worked as fast as he could, finally freeing her arms. She immediately pressed her hands against her wound as Lucas moved on to her legs.

By that time, Pete had found another knife and was working on the ropes that crossed her body. They cut and pulled until finally she was free. "Mary, don't try to get up," Lucas said to her as he fell to one knee in front of her. "Baby, just sit tight until the ambulance arrives."

He had scarcely had time to tap into his emotions, but now all those feelings slammed into him. Rage and relief, coupled with fear and love. He grabbed one of her hands, appalled to see that it was bloody from the wound. Dear God, how badly was she hurt? "Where in the hell is the ambulance?" he cried.

"It's too late. The bitch is going to die," Nicole said gleefully.

Lucas whirled around to face the old woman, who was now handcuffed. "Shut up, Nicole," he said angrily. "Just shut your damned mouth."

She looked at him in surprise. "But, Lucas, I did this for you and Diana."

"Pete, take her out of here and lock her in the back of my patrol car," Dallas said.

The minute Nicole was led away, the sound of a siren filled the air. "Hang in there, Mary. Help is on the way," Lucas said, squeezing her bloody hand.

She hung her head and continued to moan and release pitiful little cries. He couldn't stand the sound of her pain. Her tearful cries sliced straight through to his breaking heart.

Finally, the paramedics arrived. They helped her out of the chair and onto a gurney, and then she was loaded into the ambulance. The siren screamed once more as it took her away.

"I would have never suspected Nicole," Dallas said. "Thank God you decided to check out this barn." He looked at the workbench, where they saw all the items needed to make Mary a scarecrow. "And thank God you found her tonight instead of me finding her tomorrow in somebody's cornfield."

A cold shiver raced up Lucas's spine at his friend's words. He looked toward the other side of the barn, where a tarp had been thrown over what could only be a black pickup truck with front-end damage. "I forgot that Raymond had a black pickup. Nicole was the one who crashed into Mary."

He looked at his friend, suddenly stricken by a new thought. "Nicole was babysitting Annabelle the night of the crash. She must have left my little girl all alone in my house while she went after Mary. What if something had gone wrong? What if Annabelle had awakened and needed something? Thank God a fire didn't start or anything else that night."

He fisted and unfisted his hands at his sides as a new, rich anger swept through him. "I could kill her myself for putting my little girl at risk."

Dallas grabbed hold of his shoulder tightly. "Thank God nothing happened to Annabelle that night."

Some of the rage slowly left Lucas's body. "If you need me, I'll be at the hospital," Lucas said, eager to get there and find out Mary's condition. He could only hope she'd gotten to the hospital in time.

"I'll get Nicole squared away in jail, and then me and my men will probably be here most of the night processing this crime scene," Dallas replied.

"Say a prayer for Mary," Lucas said, and then he raced for his truck in the driveway.

How she must hate me now, Lucas thought as he drove to the hospital. This was all his fault. He'd lusted for Mary and, in doing so, had brought an evil madness into her life. Nicole obviously had sensed his desire for Mary. Would she even want to see him? Would she decide to leave his home and find another job?

Damn, he should have just clung to his memory of Diana. That was what he'd always intended to do.

He'd lost his way for a moment. Mary had been a sweet temptation he'd given in to. If she continued to work for him, he would never, ever give in to that temptation again.

All he wanted was for Mary to be okay. Thank God they'd found her before Nicole could have stabbed her to death. He tightened his fingers around the steering wheel, praying that Mary would survive the knife wound she'd endured.

If he thought about how afraid she must have been, how much that stabbing knife must have hurt her, he'd go stark raving mad.

He couldn't believe Nicole had such evil inside her. He'd thought he knew his mother-in-law, but he hadn't known her at all. He'd had no idea she was capable of doing something like this, that she'd harbored murder in her heart.

It had been absolutely devious of Nicole to try to take advantage of Cindy's death by making up Mary like a scarecrow to emulate her murder. It would have never worked. Dallas would have been able to figure out that it was a copycat killing.

He finally arrived at the hospital and, minutes later, was sitting in the waiting room, hoping the doctor would come out soon to tell him Mary's condition.

It all felt like horrible déjà vu. He'd sat in this very same chair the night she'd had her car accident. Nicole had tried to kill Mary that night. She'd left Annabelle alone in the house and had gone after

Mary. Mary had been incredibly lucky then. Lucas prayed she'd be incredibly lucky again tonight.

The last thing he wanted was for tonight to be the night her luck ran out. He couldn't even think such a thing. Otherwise, he'd start to cry and would never be able to stop.

The agonizing minutes ticked by. His heart raced so fast, so hard, he could hear it in his head. What was taking so long? Had she been rushed into surgery? Had the knife wound been life-threatening?

It was about two hours later when Dr. Erickson came out to talk to Lucas. "How is she?" Lucas asked as he jumped out of his chair to greet the doctor.

"That lady must have a band of angels around her," Dr. Erickson replied. "The knife missed all her vital organs. It hit her rib and went no deeper."

A shuddery relief swept through Lucas. "So she's going to be okay?"

"She has some stitches and will probably have a bruised rib—but other than that, with some time, she should be just fine," Dr. Erickson assured him.

"Can I see her?"

"I'm sorry, Lucas. I really don't think that's a good idea tonight. She's been through a terrible trauma, and I've given her some medication to help her rest. You can see her in the morning. Just know she's in good hands for tonight."

Lucas was bitterly disappointed. He'd just wanted to see her to assure himself she was really all right. "Okay, then. I'll be back tomorrow."

Lucas returned to his truck and headed back toward home. As he drove, the events of the night rushed through his head. It all felt like a dream...like a horrible, terrible nightmare. Thankfully, the end result was that Mary was alive and would be fine.

He couldn't wait to get her back home. He would care for her until she was back on her feet. He would make sure she was comfortable for as long as necessary. Then, once she was healed up, things would go back to the way they had been, only he would make sure not to cross any more boundaries.

He would once again cling tight to his memories of Diana. That was what he needed to do. He'd loved Diana, and none of this would have happened if he'd been honoring her memory the way he should have been doing.

He wanted Mary back home, giggling with Annabelle and filling the house with her warmth and sunny personality. But she would come home as his nanny and housekeeper—nothing more. His heart would forever remain with Diana.

Mary awakened to the sun shining through the window of her hospital room. Whatever the doctor had given her the night before for her anxiety and pain had made her sleep wonderfully well and without dreams.

It was only now, fully awake, that she thought about the nightmares she might have had. From the moment she'd realized Nicole had drugged her until

the moment Lucas had burst through the barn door—
everything now felt like a bad dream. But she knew
it had all been very real by the pain in her side and
the rope burns on her wrists.

Lucas. Her heart swelled with the love she felt for
him. Never had she been happier to see his beautiful face than when he'd rushed through that barn
door to save her.

Seconds before he'd rushed in, Nicole had stabbed
her. She'd been ready to stab her again when she
heard Dallas calling her name. Mary had just assumed Nicole would talk to Dallas, he'd leave and
then she'd return to finish Mary off.

In those moments, when Nicole was outside the
barn and before Lucas had come in, Mary was left
believing that, within minutes, she was going to die.
And in those final moments, she'd embraced all the
love she had for him and Annabelle in her heart.

She closed her eyes once again and tried to push
out the memories of Nicole and the abject terror she
had felt the night before. Luckily, all she felt this
morning was a bit of pain in her lower chest where
she had been stabbed and the burn of her raw wrists.

She'd just finished her breakfast when Dallas
walked into the room. "Hey, Mary, how are you doing
this morning?" He pulled a chair up next to the side
of her bed and sat.

"I'm a little sore, but other than that, I'm okay,"
she replied.

"I hate to do this to you right now, but I need to get

an official report from you about what happened last night while your memories are fresh. Do you mind if I record our conversation?" He pulled a small tape recorder out of his pocket and set it on the table between them.

"Of course I don't mind." A bit of anxiety tightened her chest as she thought of revisiting everything that had happened the night before.

"Lucas told me you had run to the grocery store to get some cookies for Annabelle. How did you wind up with Nicole?"

Mary told him about leaving the grocery store and seeing Nicole's car parked next to hers. She explained how Nicole had called her over and that when Mary slid into the passenger seat, Nicole had immediately drugged her. "I woke up tied to the chair in the barn."

Dallas continued to ask her questions about how things had unfolded from there. As Mary talked about everything, the fear from the night before crawled up her spine. It was an icy fear that gripped her insides tight and made her shiver from time to time.

"I know this is very difficult for you, Mary," he said at one point, a wealth of sympathy in his eyes. "But I need as much information as I can get to build a solid case against Nicole."

"She not only needs to go to prison, but she also needs a lot of mental help," Mary replied.

They finished up with the interview, and Dallas had just left when Dr. Reeves walked in. "Well, young lady, I'm seeing far too much of you lately."

"I definitely agree," Mary said with a smile.

"And once again, you were very lucky, my dear."

"I know. She could have easily killed me," Mary replied.

"Thank goodness she didn't," Dr. Reeves replied. He shook his head. "I've known Nicole for years, and I had no idea she was capable of such a thing."

"I think her daughter's death broke something inside her," Mary said.

"That's certainly not an excuse for what she did. Now, enough about her. Let's talk about you."

"Yes—when can I get out?"

"Are you so eager to be rid of us?" His eyes filled with a teasing light.

"It's not the company," she replied. "It's just the place."

"Thankfully, no internal damage was done. The knife wound was a clean in-and-out. The main injuries you have are seven neat little stitches, and you might have a sore rib or two. You'll also want to keep some antibacterial cream on those wounds on your wrists. We gave you a tetanus shot last night just to be on the safe side, and I've been pumping you full of antibiotics." He gestured toward the IV that was connected to the back of her hand.

"You haven't answered my question. When can I get out of here?" she repeated.

Dr. Reeves frowned. "If you feel like you're ready to get out, then I'd at least like to keep you until after lunch. Barring any complications, I suppose you can go home later this afternoon."

"Thank you, Dr. Reeves," she replied.

"And after I kick you out of here today, I'd prefer not to see you back here anytime soon."

She laughed, then groaned at the pull of her stitches. "Trust me, I'd prefer not to see you again anytime soon."

"So I'll see you after lunch," he said, and then he was gone.

Mary relaxed back against her pillow and stared out the window. There were so many thoughts tumbling around in her head. The one that continued to come to the surface was her love for Lucas.

She had never meant to fall so deeply in love with him. While she'd always found him to be a hot hunk, she certainly hadn't taken the job with the expectation of loving everything about him. She'd taken the job just wanting a decent paycheck and a working relationship with Lucas and Annabelle.

On the first day she'd gone to work for him, she'd never dreamed she'd develop such a strong, all-abiding love for him.

What had happened last night had changed things, but she wasn't sure how those things would be different. Nicole had believed Lucas was in love with her. She'd said he looked at her like he used to look at Diana.

Was it possible? Had Nicole been right? Was Lucas in love with her, and had last night finally opened his eyes to that? A shiver of delight raced through her body at the very thought. It was what she wanted more than anything—for Lucas to love her like she loved him.

Minutes later, as if conjured up by her very thoughts, Lucas walked into the room. "Sorry it took me so long to get here," he said as he grabbed a chair and pulled it up to the foot of her bed. "I had to find a babysitter for Annabelle. I didn't want to bring her with me. How are you feeling?"

His eyes were filled with deep concern and caused a wave of emotion to wash over her. She swallowed against the sudden tears. "I'm doing okay. In fact, Dr. Reeves is releasing me this afternoon."

An expression of relief filled his features. "Thank God. And thank God you weren't killed."

"Thanks to you," she replied. She smiled at him.

"Oh, Mary, I was so afraid for you." His voice cracked, and his eyes became damp. He looked away, and when he returned his gaze to her, it appeared he'd gotten himself under control.

"I'm so sorry this happened to you," he continued. "I never dreamed Nicole was so disturbed. I never dreamed you would be in any danger with her. Can you forgive me, Mary?" He looked at her intently.

"Why on earth would you need to be forgiven? You weren't the one who drugged me and then tried to kill me," she replied.

"Yes, but it was because of me it all happened in the first place," he replied, a deep regret in his voice.

"No, this happened because of Nicole. Thankfully, it's over now. Hopefully, Nicole can get the help she needs, but I also want to see her punished for what she did."

"So do I." He straightened up in the chair. "So, it's great news that you're being released later today. I'll be here to take you home, and we'll get you settled in for a few more days of rest."

"Lucas...I'm in love with you." The words whispered out of her unbidden. But the moment they left her lips, it felt right. She realized she couldn't have held them in another minute longer. She couldn't hold in her love for him another second.

He appeared positively stunned. "Mary..." He shifted uncomfortably in the chair. "I... Surely you're mistaken. After last night, you're just feeling a lot of gratitude that I got you out of Nicole's barn."

"No, it's not that. I have been in love with you for far longer than just last night," she countered. "I know what I feel, Lucas—and I'm completely and totally in love with you."

She held her breath, hoping and praying that he'd confess he was in love with her, too. She'd felt it from him. His love for her had occasionally shone in his eyes...been there in his simplest touch. Nicole hadn't been wrong, and Mary wasn't wrong. Lucas loved her; she felt it in the very depths of her heart.

He shook his head and looked away. When he gazed at her again, his features were totally emotionless, and his eyes were shuttered against her. "I told you I'm not interested in marrying again. I have my memories of my love for Diana, and that's all I need going forward. I'm hoping we can all go back to the way things were supposed to be when I first hired you. I think once we get back to that, you'll realize what you feel for me isn't love."

Each word he said pierced through her heart, into her very soul. She realized in that moment that she couldn't go back. She couldn't cook his meals and clean his house and love his daughter and pretend she didn't love him. She couldn't go back knowing that he planned on holding tight to his dead wife.

Everything had become topsy-turvy in her world. She felt as if she were back in her car and rolling upside down and downside up. But there was one thing clear in her mind: that she loved Lucas, and she believed he loved her—but he intended to turn his back on that.

She fought against the tears that burned hot in her eyes. She took a moment to get her emotions under control. "Lucas, I can't come back to work for you."

Once again, he appeared stunned. "What do you mean? Mary, please don't say that. You have to come back."

She steeled her heart against the plea in his eyes. "Lucas, I'm sorry. I know I'm leaving you in a bit of a lurch. But this afternoon, when I get out, I'm going to pack my bags and leave your house."

"Mary, please don't do that," he said with a touch of desperation in his voice. "After what you went through last night, you obviously aren't thinking clearly."

"Lucas, I'm sorry, but I have to do what's right for me. I've been thinking about it all morning, and I'm thinking clearly. I know I should have given you two weeks' notice, but last night changed everything." Once again, she bit back the tears that wanted—that *needed*—to fall.

"I…I don't even know what to say," he replied. "I hope by the time I pick you up this afternoon, you will have changed your mind."

"Actually, I'm calling Sally for a ride home. She'll bring me by your place to get my things."

His gaze searched her features. "Is there anything I can say—anything I can do—to make you stay?"

Yes—tell me you love me. Choose me instead of your memories. Please choose me. Those were the words that resonated inside her. Words she wouldn't say aloud because she had too much pride—because she wanted to hear words of love from him without her begging him.

"No," she finally answered. "I've made up my mind. Thank you for coming by to see me. I'm tired now, so I'll just see you later this afternoon." It was a not-so-subtle dismissal, and she was glad he took it as such. With a murmured goodbye and one last lingering look, he stood up and then left the room.

Once he was gone, the tears she'd fought against released. This was the hardest decision she'd ever had to make. She was walking away not only from the man she loved but also his precious daughter.

But she couldn't spend day after day in Lucas's house. She couldn't love him day after day knowing that he'd never love her back. She simply couldn't torture herself that way.

She'd get a room at the motel and go back to work at the grocery store. Life would be harder on her, but she'd never expected any different.

For a little while, she'd lived in her dream world, laughing with Lucas and playing with Annabelle. She'd thought Lucas was falling for her, and she'd seen a glimpse of what life with him would be like if he chose his love for her.

But it had only been a silly fantasy created in her mind while she'd been tied up and waiting for death. She'd believed Lucas loved her. She'd believed he was ready to build a real life with her. Realizing that wasn't true broke her.

She cried until she was left with only hiccuping sobs, and once those were gone, she called Sally for a ride. She had to walk away from him to save herself.

And that was exactly what she intended to do.

Chapter 13

When Lucas got home, he was still stunned by the idea that Mary was leaving them. He didn't care about finding a new nanny and housekeeper. He cared that Mary would no longer be in his house, making it feel like a home.

He hoped she changed her mind. God, he hoped she changed her mind. While Annabelle played in her room, Lucas sat in his recliner, trying to figure out how everything had gone so very wrong.

Mary had been saved from Nicole. He'd thought everything would go back to the way it had been before she was effectively kidnapped and stolen away.

Everything that had happened to her was because of him. Nicole had somehow sensed his lust for Mary, and it had threatened her. If he hadn't wanted Mary, none of this would have occurred.

The fact that he had been the cause of Mary's pain and terror ached inside of him. If he looked deep inside himself, he could understand why she might want to leave him and forget he had ever existed.

He'd worried that Mary would hate him, and even though she'd said she didn't blame him for what had happened, it was clear she did.

However, thinking about life without Mary was positively agonizing. She'd said she was in love with him. Was that really true? Despite his pain, the thought warmed his heart.

Was he in love with her? He honestly didn't know. All he really knew was that it didn't matter what he felt for her. He intended to go back to being a widower who held tight to the memories of his dead wife. Loving Diana felt safe.

It was four o'clock in the afternoon when a knock fell on the door. It was Mary. He hadn't said anything to Annabelle about Mary leaving because he still hoped she would change her mind and continue working for him.

But the moment he saw the strong resolve shining in her eyes, he knew she was already gone. "How are you feeling?" he asked.

"A bit sore but otherwise all right," she replied.

"Ms. Mary." Annabelle came running in from her room. "Daddy said you have more boo-boos. Want me to kiss them better?"

"No, sweetheart," Mary replied. "My boo-boos are already getting better." She looked back at him. "It won't take me long." She then headed down the hallway toward the room where she had been staying.

He had a wild desire to chase after her, to bar the bedroom door so she couldn't get in to pack and leave. Of course, he did neither of those things. He merely stood at the end of the hallway as a deep grief ripped through him.

He couldn't believe this was really happening or how much it hurt. He would no longer share laughter with her in the evenings. He would no longer be greeted by her sunshine smile when he came in from working the fields. He would never again smell the evocative scent of her lilac-based perfume.

The house would go back to a certain kind of darkness without her in it. Annabelle would be brokenhearted—*he* would be brokenhearted. But he didn't have any idea how to stop this all from happening. He sank down on the sofa and dropped his head into his hands.

Right now, his daughter was playing in her bedroom, unaware that not only was his world about to change but hers as well. Now his heart ached for the loss his little girl would feel without her beloved Ms. Mary.

About fifteen minutes later, Annabelle came running out of her bedroom. She carried a baby doll in each arm. "Play with me, Daddy?" Annabelle asked.

"Baby, I don't want to play right now. But I need

to talk to you," he said, pulling her little body closer to him. "Ms. Mary isn't going to live here with us anymore. She's going away tonight."

Annabelle frowned. "Why, Daddy?"

Why indeed. He wasn't even sure how to answer her. He didn't want to talk to her about adult issues. At least he was saved from having to say anything since Mary was coming down the hallway, dragging her two suitcases behind her.

He jumped up to help her with the biggest one. He pulled it to the front door. "I still need to get the box," she said and disappeared back down the hallway. A moment later, she carried the box out to the front door and set it down. "I think that's everything," she said.

"Ms. Mary, Ms. Mary!" Annabelle launched herself at Mary and wrapped her arms around her waist. "Don't go away, Ms. Mary." As Annabelle began to cry, Mary leaned down to Annabelle's level. "Don't you love me anymore, Ms. Mary? I love you. Don't you love me?"

"Oh, honey, I will always love you," Mary said. Tears filled her eyes as she pulled Annabelle into her arms for a tight hug.

"Don't go, Ms. Mary. 'Kay? Don't go." Again, Annabelle grabbed Mary around the waist.

Mary closed her eyes and began to cry. A wealth of emotion filled Lucas as he watched the two saying goodbye. Surely Annabelle's tears would move Mary to change her mind.

Mary opened her tear-filled eyes and unwound

Annabelle's arms. "I have to go, Annabelle," Mary said. "But you'll see me again at the grocery store."

"No, I want to see you here," Annabelle cried.

Mary picked up her two suitcases. "I have to go now. Honey, please stop crying."

"Five more minutes, 'kay? Stay five more minutes," Annabelle begged. Mary looked at Lucas, her eyes filled with tears.

"Five more minutes." Annabelle started to follow Mary out the front door.

"Come here, baby." Lucas scooped up his daughter in his arms, where she buried her face in his shoulder and continued to cry.

Mary got her suitcases out the door, and then she picked up the box and took it outside as well. Once everything was outside, she closed the door after her.

She was gone. She was really gone, leaving behind a brokenhearted little girl and a man who already missed her.

Sally helped Mary get her things into the motel room where she would be staying until she found something better. "Lordy, Mary. This place is absolutely horrible," Sally said. She had helped Mary load her things into the back of Mary's car and then she had followed Mary here to help her get everything into the room.

"It will be fine. It just needs to be spruced up some," Mary replied.

"No amount of 'sprucing up' is going to make this room less dismal," Sally replied with a deep frown.

"It will be fine because it has to be fine for now," Mary said, fighting back tears of heartbreak, pain and exhaustion.

"I wish I had an extra bedroom," Sally said. "I'd move you in with me."

Mary smiled at her friend. "I'll be okay, Sally. Thank goodness I got my job back at the grocery store. I'll look for someplace else to rent in the next few days or so."

"Mary, I hope you're planning to take time to rest. Remember, you just got out of the hospital this afternoon after being stabbed and terrorized."

"I'm taking the next week to rest. Thank you for helping me today, Sally. Now, get out of here so I can unpack and get settled in."

Sally gave her an uncertain look. "You'll call me if you need anything?"

"I promise I will."

The minute Sally left, Mary sat down on the edge of the double bed and fought back tears. These motel rooms were rarely rented by tourists. One of the units had been rented for years by Rocky Landow, a veteran who had lost a leg serving the country. He was a nice man who kept to himself and caused no problems for anyone.

Another one of the units was rented by Burt Ramsey, the town drunk who made just enough money doing odd jobs to rent the room and buy himself plenty of alcohol.

And then there was this unit, which Mary had rented out for the next two weeks. The double bed was covered with a worn gold bedspread, and a small television was bolted to the top of a dresser. The tops of the nightstands were cigarette-burned and polka-dotted with dozens of rings left behind by dozens of drinks.

There was a small kitchenette with a refrigerator, a stove and a sink. There was also a microwave on top of the kitchen countertop.

It was a far cry from the beautiful room she'd had at Lucas's place. She squeezed her eyes closed for a moment. She couldn't think of Lucas or Anna-belle right now. If she did, she would break down completely.

She got up from the bed and opened the suitcase that held her toiletries and nightclothes. She carried her bag of toiletries into the small bathroom. At least everything looked relatively clean.

She returned to her suitcase and pulled out a few things to hang in the closet. Once she'd done that, she went back into the bathroom and stripped off the clothes she'd been wearing throughout her ordeal with Nicole. She hadn't had an opportunity to change yet today. She threw the clothes into the wastebasket and then started the shower.

Thankfully, the shower spray was strong and the

water was nice and hot. It was as she stood beneath the water that her tears began to fall once again.

As she thought of Annabelle's tears, Mary cried harder. Saying goodbye to the little girl she loved had been far more difficult than she'd expected. And saying goodbye to Lucas had been utterly heartbreaking.

She'd had such hope that Lucas would be in love with her, that he'd profess that love and they could live happily ever after.

She could have sworn she'd seen his love for her shining from his eyes. She'd believed that the lengths he went to last night to find her had been a testament of his love for her.

But she would not live beneath the shadow of a dead woman. She understood and respected that he had loved Diana; she didn't want to take anything away from that. She'd just wanted him to choose a future and not the past.

It didn't matter now. None of it mattered. It was done and over, and now she was back to figuring out what her future would be. But not tonight.

She got out of the shower and pulled on her nightshirt. Tonight, she intended to take one of the pain pills the doctor had prescribed for her and go to bed. Hopefully, she would sleep without dreams and without the grief that still ripped through her as she thought of Lucas and Annabelle.

Lucas would certainly be all right because he was in charge of his life and his choices. Annabelle would also be okay. She was young—and probably within weeks, she'd have a new nanny and forget all about Ms. Mary.

After taking her pill, Mary curled up beneath the sheets that smelled of comforting laundry detergent and bleach. How long would it take for her to forget how much she loved Annabelle? How much she loved Lucas?

For a little while, they had been her family, and she had felt that warmth—the love of family. It had been something she'd never, ever felt before…and she feared that she would never, ever feel that way again.

She cried herself to sleep and awoke to morning sunshine creeping in around the blinds at the window. Her eyes felt swollen, her body ached, the wound beneath her breast burned and hurt, and her heart still felt as broken as it had the night before.

She didn't feel like doing anything productive at all. But she did need to get to the grocery store to get some supplies and food to eat.

With this goal in mind, she dressed in a pair of jeans and a T-shirt and headed out. It was early enough in the morning that the store was nearly deserted. The only people she saw were a couple of her coworkers.

She bought what she thought she would need for a week or so and then returned to the motel to unload the items. Once everything was put away, she made herself a pot of coffee and warmed up a bagel in the oven, then got back into the bed with the television on.

She was hoping to keep her mind as empty as possible. She just wanted to rest and heal—not only for her physical injuries but also her grief.

But it was difficult to keep her mind empty when it was so filled with memories of Lucas and Annabelle, and all her memories were happy ones.

She almost wished she and Lucas had had a horrible fight and he had thrown her out. Then she might have wound up disliking him. But there had been no fight—not even a cross word between them.

He probably hated her now. She'd left him in a lurch, with nobody to care for Annabelle so he could work in the fields. She hoped he found somebody to quickly fill her position. The idea of another woman in the house, taking care of Lucas and Annabelle, sent a stabbing shaft of pain through her heart.

For the next three days, she stayed in bed, watching television and napping off and on. On the morning of the fourth day, she once again dressed to head back to the grocery store for a few more items.

Physically, she felt considerably better; but mentally, she was still grieving. It was going to take her a very long time to get over loving Lucas.

Once she got to the store, she immediately headed to the canned-vegetable-and-soup aisle. She was in the mood for some tomato and chicken noodle soup. Wasn't it supposed to be good for the soul?

She was bending down to grab a couple of cans when she heard her name. She straightened up to see Lucas hurrying toward her. What was he doing?

What did he want? He looked tired. She steeled her heart, needing to wrap herself in a shield of defensiveness against him.

"Mary, thank God I found you. I was on my way to the motel to talk to you but saw your car parked outside here."

"Did I leave something at your house?" She couldn't think of any other reason he would be looking for her.

"Yes." His eyes gazed into hers intently. "Yes, you left behind the echoes of your laughter and the great conversations we shared. Mary, you left behind the memories of happiness in my home, of making love to you and so much more. Oh, Mary, I've been such a fool."

She stared at him, unsure of what was happening even as a small nugget of hope lit up in her heart. "You've been a fool?"

"Completely. I couldn't wait to get home after work because I knew you would be there. I loved sitting across the table from you as we ate dinner. I love the sound of your laughter and the way you love my daughter. Hell, I even love the way you smell. Come home, Mary. Come back to where you belong."

He stepped closer to her and took her hands in his. "Mary, I'm miserable without you. I'm so in love with you, and I don't want to live in the past anymore." He tightened his hold on her hands. "Come home. I want to marry you and build a life with you."

"Say that again," she said as a happiness she'd never known swelled in her heart.

He dropped her hands and pulled her into an embrace. "I'm in love with you, Mary. Please marry me and make me the happiest man in the world."

"Yes, oh yes," she said, and she could say no more, as his lips claimed hers in a kiss that spoke of love and laughter and a wonderful future.

When the kiss finally ended, she looked up at him with a smile. "Five more minutes, 'kay? Kiss me for five more minutes."

He laughed with obvious delight. "It would be my pleasure." And he proceeded to do just that.

Epilogue

It was a Friday evening, and they were all having dinner in the café. Mary had moved her things back to the farm—the only difference was she now spent her nights in Lucas's bed.

For the past week since she'd moved back in, life had been beyond wonderful. Lucas and Annabelle were definitely her family, and she couldn't be happier.

"I want mashed taters and chocolate cake and french fries and spaghetti," Annabelle said as they settled into a booth.

Lucas and Mary laughed. "How about you get spaghetti and meatballs and have chocolate cake for dessert?" Mary suggested. "And if you want some french fries, I'll share some of mine."

The little girl nodded with a smile. "'Kay," she agreed.

"That was easy enough," Lucas said with a warm smile of his own.

"Sharing french fries is always a good thing," Mary replied.

As usual, there was a large crowd in the café, and when they'd walked in, Mary had been greeted by many well-wishers. Everyone in town had heard of her ordeal at the hands of Nicole, and the support Mary had received was amazing and wonderful.

The waitress appeared at their table, and they placed their orders. "Annabelle, we're happy that Mary is going to be in our lives forever, right?" Lucas asked as soon as the waitress left.

"Forever and ever," Annabelle replied. She reached for Mary's hand and squeezed tightly. "You aren't going to leave us again. Right, Ms. Mary?"

"I'm never, ever going to leave you again, sweetheart," Mary replied.

"And I'm going to make sure that she's never going to leave us again," Lucas said and slid out of the booth.

He moved to stand in front of Mary. "What are you doing, Lucas?" A nervous little laugh escaped her. Oh, when he looked at her the way he was looking at her now, she felt as if she was the most beautiful woman in the world.

He smiled at her. "Mary, I love you with all my heart," he said. He pulled her up out of the booth. "And I think it's time we make it official." He fell to one knee in the aisle, and for a moment, the entire café seemed to quiet.

Mary's heart pounded as he took a small box out of his pocket. "Mary Curtis, will you please marry us?" He opened the box to reveal a beautiful princess-cut diamond ring.

It wouldn't have mattered if it had been a ring out of a gumball machine. "Yes, Lucas. Of course yes," she replied as tears of joy blurred her vision.

He took her hand and slid the ring on her finger, and the crowd in the café erupted in cheers. "Ms. Mary, Ms. Mary," Annabelle yelled to be heard over the noise. The crowd hushed. "Ms. Mary, Daddy said I can call you Mommy. Is that okay with you, Ms. Mary? I love you so much, and I want you to be my mommy."

New tears filled Mary's eyes at the little girl's words. "Oh, sweetheart, I would love it if you'd call me Mommy," she replied.

There would be a time to make Annabelle really understand about the mother she had lost, but that would come later. For now, the fact that Annabelle wanted to give Mary that title filled her heart with sheer joy.

Lucas pulled Mary into his arms. "Now that we're officially engaged, we need to plan the wedding of your dreams," he said.

"All I need is you and Annabelle and a preacher," she replied. "That will make it the wedding of my dreams."

The crowd cheered again as he leaned down and captured her lips in a kiss that spoke of love and commitment and a happily-ever-after life. Mary finally had a real family of her own, and her heart swelled with a happiness she knew she'd feel for the rest of her life.

His basement smelled of blood and death, and he loved it. He was the talk of the town for a while when Cindy had been found on a stake in Lucas's cornfield. However, the kidnapping and near-murder of Mary Curtis had kicked him right out of the gossip mill.

Now he was ready to get everyone talking about him again. He looked over to the workbench, where jeans and a flannel shirt sat next to a straw hat. Ready for his next victim.

The only remnant he had of his last scarecrow was a jar of alcohol containing Cindy's eyes. He'd hoped they would keep their bright blue color, but to his disappointment, they had turned a milky white.

His gaze fell once again on the items he had to make his next scarecrow. All he had to do was decide who would be his second victim.

Then the town would once again talk about him... *fear* him. Hopefully, it would earn him an official name. He already had one for himself: the Scarecrow Killer. Once he had an official name and continued on his path, then he'd go down in history as a man who killed dozens of women and turned them into human scarecrows…a killer who had never been caught.

Chills of delight shook through his body. Yes, it was time for the Scarecrow Killer to act again.

* * * * *

*For a sneak peek at the next story in
Carla Cassidy's exciting new miniseries,
The Scarecrow Murders, turn the page...*

Chapter 1

Harper Brennan sat on her sofa and stared at the birthday cake on the coffee table. The cake was a beautiful dark chocolate, frosted with a rich raspberry buttercream and baked in her very own bakery, the Sweet Tooth.

She'd planned a very small birthday party for herself tonight with two of her best friends. Unfortunately, they had both canceled at the last minute. So now Harper was having a pity party for one, and she was the guest of honor.

She grabbed one of the silly pointed party hats she'd bought, fastened it atop her head and stared at the single candle in the center of the cake. There was only one candle because there was no way the cake could hold forty-five.

Forty-five. She'd never thought she would be celebrating a birthday alone at this age. Six years ago, she'd been happily married and was dreaming of opening her own bakery.

She'd managed to see her dream of the bakery come true, but her marriage had ended when her husband left her for a twenty-five-year-old woman. Jerk. At least the happy couple had moved away so Harper didn't have to see them every day.

She now sighed and picked up a lighter to light the single candle. In the mood she was in, she felt like bingeing on cake, eating half of it or more. But she'd only eat a small piece because lately it seemed she only had to look at food, and extra pounds jumped right to her tummy and hips.

Before she could light the candle, a knock sounded at her door. Maybe one of her friends had made it after all. She jumped up off the sofa and hurried to the front door. She opened it to see Sam Bravano standing on her porch.

"Hi, Harper. I'm here about the ad." He smiled, revealing a dimple in one cheek.

Sam Bravano. She'd seen him around town many times, but nothing had prepared her for seeing him up close and personal.

Lordy, if she were ten years younger, she'd jump his bones. And fine bones they were. With his broad shoulders; slim hips; dark, slightly shaggy hair; and his unexpected yet vivid green eyes, he was definitely a piece of eye candy.

"Harper?" His smile faltered, and she realized she'd just been standing there staring at him and maybe mentally drooling a bit. God, she hoped she hadn't really been drooling.

"Oh, yes…the ad. Uh, come on in." She opened the door wider to allow him entry. As he passed her, she caught the scent of sunshine, a hint of spicy cologne and intoxicating male.

"Please, have a seat." She gestured toward the chair facing the sofa.

"It's your birthday?" he asked as he sat.

"It is. Would you like a piece of cake? I'd planned a little party for myself with a couple of friends, but at the last minute, they couldn't make it."

"It's no fun to celebrate your birthday all alone." He stood, and to her utter surprise, he grabbed one of the party hats from the coffee table and put it on his head.

Even the silly hat didn't detract from his attractiveness.

The man definitely knew how to wear a pair of worn jeans and a T-shirt. He was tanned and incredibly fit.

Harper sank back down on the sofa. "I was just about to light the candle when you knocked on the door."

"Then by all means, light the candle," he replied,

that charming dimple winking at her once again. "How many other candles should there be?"

She laughed. "Enough to burn this house down." She lit the candle.

"Now, wait to blow it out," Sam said. "What's supposed to happen now is everyone sings 'Happy Birthday.' So here goes…" To her surprise again, he stood up and began to sing the traditional song.

His lovely baritone not only filled the room but shot warmth straight through her. She swallowed against unexpected tears. He was obviously being very kind to a lonely older woman. "Now, make a wish and blow out your candle," he said when he finished singing.

She made her wish and blew out the candle. "You can take off that silly hat now," she said as she took off the one on her head. She picked up the cake server, cut a liberal piece, placed it on one of her decorative plates and held it out toward him.

He swept the hat off his head and took the cake. "Wow, this looks delicious."

"I hope it is." She handed him a fork.

"Aren't you having a piece?" he asked.

"I'll, uh, have one later. You said you were here about the ad. Sam, I know your work around town, and I know you've seen my storefront. It obviously needs a lot of work."

She'd gotten an amazing price on the piece of real estate on Main Street because it had needed a lot of cosmetic work. Since opening the business a little over two years ago, she'd focused most of her work and finances on the inside. Now she had enough money saved and a small loan in place to begin work on the outside.

She'd placed an ad requesting a carpenter in the local *Millsville News*. Sam and his two brothers were all carpenters who often worked at one project or another around town.

"It just needs a bit of a face-lift," Sam replied.

Yeah, that makes two of us, she thought wryly. "I'd like to do a bit more than a face-lift in the back." As she told him her plans, he set aside his half-eaten cake and pulled out a notepad and pen from his back pocket and made notes.

She was acutely aware of him. She'd had men in her living room before, but none of them had filled the space quite like he did. Even sitting, energy wafted from him. Yet it wasn't an uncomfortable energy; rather, it was soft and soothing and would instantly put a person at ease.

And yet she felt oddly on edge. Maybe it was because of the way he looked at her so intently, like what she said was the most important thing in the world. Or maybe it was because he exuded a self-confidence and strength in a quiet way. Then there was that dimple…

Oh, the young ladies in town must be positively mad about Sam.

"Business must be good for you to plan all these

renovations," he said. He picked up his piece of cake once again.

"It helps to be the only bakery in town," she replied.

"There is that," he agreed with a grin. "But from what I've heard, you're good at what you do. And if this cake is any indication, you're *damn* good at what you do."

She felt a blush warm her cheeks. "Thanks."

"Did you always want to be a baker?"

The personal question surprised her. "From the time I was little, I liked to bake and dreamed of having a place where I could sell my goodies to other people. My mom loved to bake, too, and we often worked together in the kitchen."

A quick wave of sadness fluttered through her. She'd lost her mother the year before to a heart attack. Three years after her father had passed from the same ailment.

"Did you always want to be a carpenter?"

"My dad was a carpenter all his life, and I often went to jobs with him. I wanted to follow in his footsteps. Besides, I enjoy working hard and then seeing something tangible. I enjoy building something new or rebuilding something old." He laughed. "And that was probably more than you wanted to hear."

"Not at all," she protested. "I've always been interested in what people do and why." She shrugged and felt a blush once again heat her cheeks. "I guess I've always been a people person."

"That's a good thing, right?" He smiled at her.

She held his gaze for a long moment and then looked down at the cake. "So, what happens now?" She looked up at him once again.

"What I'd like to do is come to the bakery tomorrow morning and take some measurements and check things out. It's the only way I can give you a close estimate as to what all this is going to cost," Sam said, pulling her from her momentary sad thoughts. "Will nine o'clock work for you?"

"That would be fine," she agreed.

He stood up. "I would encourage you to get several estimates, but I'm betting I can beat anyone else's price, and I definitely do better work than anyone else in town." His green eyes sparkled brightly at his last words.

She got up as well and walked with him to the front door. He was a tall drink of water and towered over her. She opened the door and then gazed up at him. "Thank you, Sam, for sharing my birthday with me."

He smiled. "It was my pleasure, Harper. I'll see you tomorrow."

Good Lordy, the man looked as good going as he had coming. When he reached his pickup truck in the driveway, she closed her door and locked it.

As she carried the cake and then the dirty dishes to the kitchen, she thought about Sam's suggestion that she get estimates from other places. She didn't intend to waste her time.

She'd spoken to several people who'd had work done by Sam and his brothers, and everyone had said they were hardworking, delivered on time and had been very fair with their prices. So why get other estimates?

She sat at the kitchen table with a small slice of cake before her. It was a slow time at the bakery right now. The Fourth of July had passed, and the next big holiday was months away. Thank goodness she had regular customers who came in daily for coffee and a cinnamon roll, a slice of cake or cookies.

The cake was delicious, and once she'd put it into the refrigerator, she headed for her bedroom even though it was relatively early. Bedtime always came early for her because she started in the bakery at five in the mornings.

Once she was in bed, she couldn't help but think about Sam. He seemed like a nice guy. She guessed he was around thirty years old. Too bad he wasn't ten years older.

She turned over on her back and stared up at the ceiling, where shadows from the moonlight danced. She wouldn't mind having a man in her life again. She missed eating dinner with somebody. She missed intriguing conversations and laughter. She missed watching a sunrise or a sunset with a special some- body.

She finally fell asleep and into totally inappropri- ate and delicious dreams of Sam Bravano.

* * *

Sam whistled as he left Harper's place. The cake was still a delicious taste in his mouth, and the woman who had baked it intrigued him.

She was a cute little thing with short, curly dark hair and bright blue eyes. She had captured his attention more than once whenever he saw her out and about in town.

It had definitely been kind of pathetic to walk in on her having a birthday party all alone. She'd looked charming even with the silly party hat atop her curls. He had no idea what had possessed him to sing to her. It had just felt like the right thing to do in the moment.

He pulled away from her house and headed home. As he drove down the main drag of the small town of Millsville, Kansas, a sense of pride filled him. He loved this town, and he had worked on several of the storefronts, transforming them from old, tired facades into colorful places that breathed new life.

He wasn't surprised when he pulled up in his driveway to see his two younger brothers lounging in the two wicker chairs on the front porch. Tony and Michael almost looked like twins, despite there being two years between them. They sat up straight in their chairs when they saw him.

Sam had bought the two-story house a year ago. It had needed a lot of work, and his idea was to get it back into good shape and either remain in it or flip it, depending on what the housing market was doing when he got it finished.

Because his two brothers still lived at home, they often popped in at his house in the evenings. Tony wasn't dating anyone in particular at the moment, and Michael had an on-again, off-again girlfriend named Paula.

"Good evening, boys," he said as he approached them.

"Hey, Sam," Tony said and got up from his chair.

"Where have you been?" Michael asked, rising from his own chair.

"Since when do I need to check in with you?" Sam asked good-naturedly as he unlocked his front door.

"Just wondering, that's all," Michael replied as he and Tony followed Sam through the front door. Tony made a beeline for the kitchen and reappeared a moment later with three beers in hand.

He tossed one to Michael, who had reseated himself on Sam's sofa, and then one to Sam, who eased down in his recliner. "So, what's new?" Sam asked once they were all seated with beers cracked open.

"Paula and I broke up again last night," Michael said.

"Have you ever considered that maybe she's not the right one for you?" Sam asked.

"But I'm crazy about her," Michael lamented.

"You're a schmuck," Tony said. "That girl leads you around like a puppy dog. When she snaps her fingers, you jump. You need to get better game, bro."

"What he needs is a better girlfriend," Sam observed.

As his two brothers complained and moaned about their love lives, Sam silently sipped his beer. Sam was ten years older than Michael and eight years older than Tony.

At thirty-three years old, Sam had been through the romance wringer. He'd dated often and had dated a lot of women but hadn't found that special someone. Lately, he'd felt a quiet desperation wafting from the women he dated—the desperation to get married and have babies.

While Sam would love to find a woman who would want to share his life with him, he'd never really wanted children, and he wasn't even sure the whole marriage thing was for him.

Of course, his mother was on him all the time about grandbabies, but he figured his brothers or his older sister could fulfill that wish for their mother.

"So, really… Where were you this evening, Sam?" Michael asked again when the conversation about their love lives had waned.

"I answered Harper Brennan's ad in the paper for a carpenter. She wants to have a little work done at the Sweet Tooth," Sam replied.

"Does that mean we all have a new job?" Tony asked. "We've still got to finish up the gazebo in the town square." Several weeks ago, the members of the town council had hired them to build a gazebo that people in town could enjoy.

"There isn't that much left to do on that job. I figure you two, along with Bud and Aaron, can finish it up," Sam replied. Bud Kurtz and Aaron Palmer were a couple of teenagers who were always up for earning extra money by working for the Bravano brothers.

"What exactly does Harper want done?" Tony asked.

"I'm not sure. I'm meeting her in the morning to discuss things. From what little she already told me, I should be able to handle a lot of it on my own. However, I might need you two to help me there in a few weeks," Sam said.

He found it odd that, for some reason, he was reluctant to share with his brothers too much about his time spent with Harper this evening. He also found it odd that he was reluctant to have them working with him there, at least initially.

"Have you heard if Dallas has any more clues in Cindy's murder?" Tony asked, changing the subject.

"That was creepy as hell," Michael said darkly.

"As far as I've heard, he's no closer to finding her murderer," Sam replied.

It had been almost a month since the body of Cindy Perry, a young woman who had worked as a waitress at the café, had been found in Lucas Maddox's cornfield. She'd been trussed up on a pole like a human scarecrow. Her mouth had been sewn shut, and her eyes were missing.

Dallas Calloway, the chief of police, had quickly let it be known that Lucas wasn't a suspect; unfortunately, there didn't seem to be *any* viable suspects. The murder had definitely cast a pall over the town.

Thankfully, his brothers didn't stay long, and the next morning at quarter till nine, he pulled up and parked in front of the Sweet Tooth Bakery.

The bakery was located on Main Street, and Harper's house was less than a block away. The commercial building had rotting boards and was painted a fading, tired brown. The only saving grace was the large bright pink sign that hung over the doorway. It not only had the name of the place on it but also a cupcake with white icing and pink sprinkles.

The sign could remain, but most all the wood on the front either needed to be replaced or painted. The air just outside of the building smelled mouthwatering.

He'd never been in the business before even though he enjoyed cakes and cookies and such. But his mother baked goodies regularly, so he'd never felt the need to go into the bakery.

He entered the front door and stepped inside. In here, the scents were even more delicious. Directly ahead of him was a long display counter holding beautiful cakes, cupcakes and a variety of cookies. A coffee machine was behind the counter—one of those fancy ones that spewed out straight coffee or cappuccino or hot chocolate.

There were several high round-topped tables with pink-and-white-striped chairs. The walls were white with pink trim, on which were several large photos depicting cakes he assumed Harper had baked. Harper was nowhere to be seen, but there was a bell on the counter, and so he rang it.

She came through a doorway that led to the back. She was clad in a pair of jeans that hugged her legs and a blue blouse that did amazing things to her blue eyes. Over it all, she had on a blue-and-white apron that was sporting a bit of flour.

"Sam, sorry I didn't hear you come in," she said.

"It's okay. I've just been looking around. It's quite inviting in here."

"Thanks. It's a total disconnect from the outside, right?"

"Right, but we're going to fix that," he said confidently. "We'll make sure the outside is as inviting as the inside."

"That's the plan," she agreed.

"I just wanted to let you know I was here and that I'll be outside doing some measuring, and then later I'll come back in and give you an estimate."

"That sounds perfect to me," she agreed. "I'm really looking forward to getting the process started." Her eyes sparkled brightly. God, she had pretty eyes, with long dark lashes.

"Then I'll see you back here in about twenty minutes." With a smile, he turned and left the shop. He whistled as he walked back to his truck and retrieved his tape measure and a small pad and pen.

Before he could start measuring, Joe Rogers approached the shop. "Hey, Joe. How's life?" Sam greeted him. Sam would guess that Joe was in his late fifties or early sixties. He was divorced and lived on a small farm at the edge of town.

"It's going," Joe replied. "Although, my days don't really begin until I get a cup of coffee and one of Harper's big cinnamon rolls. Looks like she's finally ready to do something to spruce up the place."

"That's why I'm here," Sam replied. "See you later, Joe, and enjoy your cinnamon roll."

"I always do," the man said and then disappeared into the bakery.

It was twenty minutes later when Sam reentered the shop. Joe was seated at one of the tables, and Harper stood behind her display case. Sam walked up to her. "I'd like a cup of black coffee and one of your cinnamon rolls. Then, whenever you're ready to talk, I'm ready." He pulled out his wallet.

"Put that away," she said. "It's on the house this morning."

"Is that because you like me?" he teased.

"No... I mean, yes..." Her cheeks turned a charming pink. "Why don't you have a seat at one of the tables, and I'll be right with you."

"Harper, I'm taking off," Joe said. "I'll see you tomorrow."

"Okay, Joe," she replied.

As Joe left, Harper carried the coffee and the cinnamon roll to where Sam sat. She set the things on the table and then took a seat across from him. "So, what have you got for me?"

"This is only an estimate on the front. You'll need to walk out back with me to show me what you want specifically out there," he explained.

As he went over the supplies and the cost, he was only interrupted once when Letta Lee, president of the gardening club, came in.

Letta was a sixtysomething-year-old woman who Sam believed was one of the most judgmental snobs in town. She was also known to be a big gossip. Thankfully, she picked up a cake she'd ordered and then left.

"So when can you start?" Harper asked when she rejoined him at the table.

"As soon as you want," he replied.

"As soon as you can," she said.

Minutes later, the financial aspect of the job had been hammered out, and Sam left to head to the lumberyard to arrange the supplies he would need.

He was eager to get started on the job, and he was even more eager to get to know Harper better. For the first time in a long time, a woman interested and attracted him.

He wasn't sure what it was about her, but he felt a spark with her, and he couldn't wait to explore it…and her.

The Trouble with Sam *by Carla Cassidy, coming soon from Harlequin Romantic Suspense!*

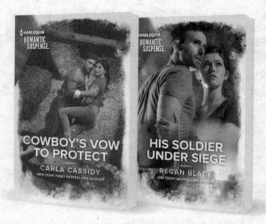

#2207 TO TRUST A COLTON COWBOY
The Coltons of Colorado • by Dana Nussio

Jasper Colton could never act on his crush—not only is Kayla St. James his employee, but his father's corruption sent her dad to prison. And yet he can't help but step in when she's dealing with a stalker. As the threats escalate, the two of them find their attraction hard to resist.

#2208 IN THE ARMS OF THE LAW
To Serve and Seduce • by Deborah Fletcher Mello

Attorney Ellington Black will sacrifice everything for his family. But when his brother is charged with murder, Special Agent Angela Stanfield puts his loyalty to the test. As her investigation puts her in danger—and points to a different killer than his brother—Ellington finds himself in the role of protector...and desire turns to love!

#2209 HOTSHOT HEROES UNDER THREAT
Hotshot Heroes • by Lisa Childs

Hotshot firefighter Patrick McRooney goes undercover to find the saboteur on his brother-in-law's elite Hotshot team, but as his investigation gets closer to the truth—and he gets closer to Henrietta Rowlins—threats are made. And Patrick isn't the only one they're targeting...

#2210 TEXAS LAW: UNDERCOVER JUSTICE
Texas Law • by Jennifer D. Bokal

Clare Chambers is a woman on the run and Isaac Patton is undercover, trying to find a hit man. When a body is found in the small town of Mercy, Texas, the two have to work together to catch a killer before Clare becomes the next victim.

HRSCNM1022

The whole desperate plan began simply as a last-ditch attempt to save his life. He never intended for anyone to get hurt. That day, not long after Thanksgiving, he walked into the bank full of hope. It was the first time he'd ever asked for a loan. It was also the first time he'd ever seen executive loan officer Carla Richmond.

When he tapped at her open doorway, she looked up from that big desk of hers. He thought she was too young and pretty with her big blue eyes and all that curly chestnut-brown hair to make the decision as to whether he lived or died.

She had a great smile as she got to her feet to offer him a seat.

He felt so out of place in her plush office that he stood in the doorway nervously kneading the brim of his worn baseball cap for a moment before stepping in. As he did, her blue-eyed gaze took in his ill-fitting clothing hanging on his rangy body, his bad haircut, his large, weathered hands.

He told himself that she'd already made up her mind before he even sat down. She didn't give men like him a second look—let alone money. Like his father always said, bankers never gave dough to poor people who actually needed it. They just helped their rich friends.

Right away Carla Richmond made him feel small with her questions about his employment record, what he had for collateral, why he needed the money and how he planned to repay it. He'd recently lost one crappy job and was in the process of starting another temporary one, and all he had to show for the years he'd worked hard labor since high school was an old pickup and a pile of bills.

He took the forms she handed him and thanked her, knowing he wasn't going to bother filling them in. On the way out of her office, he balled them up and dropped them in the trash. All the way to his pickup, he mentally kicked himself for being such a fool. What had he expected?

No one was going to give him money, even to save his life—especially some woman in a suit behind a big desk in an air-conditioned office. It didn't matter that she didn't have a clue how desperate he really was. All she'd seen when she'd looked at him was a loser. To think that he'd bought a new pair of jeans with the last of his cash and borrowed a too-large button-up shirt from a former coworker for this meeting.

After climbing into his truck, he sat for a moment, too scared and sick at heart to start the engine. The worst part was the thought of going home and telling Jesse. The way his luck was going, she would walk out on him. Not that he could blame her, since his gambling had gotten them into this mess.

He thought about blowing off work, since his new job was only temporary anyway, and going straight to the bar. Then he reminded himself that he'd spent the last of his money on the jeans. He couldn't even afford a beer. His own fault, he reminded himself. He'd only made things worse when he'd gone to a loan shark for cash and then stupidly gambled the money, thinking he could make back what he owed and then some when he won. He'd been so sure his luck had changed for the better when he'd met Jesse.

Last time the two thugs had come to collect the interest on the loan, they'd left him bleeding in the dirt outside his rented house. They would be back any day.

With a curse, he started the pickup. A cloud of exhaust blew out the back as he headed home to face Jesse with the bad news. Asking for a loan had been a long shot, but still he couldn't help thinking about the disappointment he'd see in her eyes when he told her. They'd planned to go out tonight for an expensive dinner with the loan money to celebrate.

As he drove home, his humiliation began to fester like a sore that just wouldn't heal. Had he known even then how this was going to end? Or was he still telling himself he was just a nice guy who'd made some mistakes, had some bad luck and gotten involved with the wrong people?

Don't miss
Christmas Ransom *by B.J. Daniels,*
available December 2022 wherever
Harlequin books and ebooks are sold.

Harlequin.com

Get 4 FREE REWARDS!

We'll send you 2 FREE Books plus 2 FREE Mystery Gifts.

FREE Value Over **$20**

Both the **Harlequin Intrigue®** and **Harlequin® Romantic Suspense** series feature compelling novels filled with heart-racing action-packed romance that will keep you on the edge of your seat.

YES! Please send me 2 FREE novels from the Harlequin Intrigue or Harlequin Romantic Suspense series and my 2 FREE gifts (gifts are worth about $10 retail). After receiving them, if I don't wish to receive any more books, I can return the shipping statement marked "cancel." If I don't cancel, I will receive 6 brand-new Harlequin Intrigue Larger-Print books every month and be billed just $6.24 each in the U.S. or $6.74 each in Canada, a savings of at least 14% off the cover price or 4 brand-new Harlequin Romantic Suspense books every month and be billed just $5.24 each in the U.S. and $5.99 each in Canada, a savings of at least 13% off the cover price. It's quite a bargain! Shipping and handling is just 50¢ per book in the U.S. and $1.25 per book in Canada.* I understand that accepting the 2 free books and gifts places me under no obligation to buy anything. I can always return a shipment and cancel at any time by calling the number below. The free books and gifts are mine to keep no matter what I decide.

Choose one: ☐ **Harlequin Intrigue**
   Larger-Print
   (199/399 HDN GRA2)

☐ **Harlequin Romantic Suspense**
(240/340 HDN GRCE)

Name (please print)

Address   Apt. #

City   State/Province   Zip/Postal Code

Email: Please check this box ☐ if you would like to receive newsletters and promotional emails from Harlequin Enterprises ULC and its affiliates. You can unsubscribe anytime.

Mail to the Harlequin Reader Service:
IN U.S.A.: P.O. Box 1341, Buffalo, NY 14240-8531
IN CANADA: P.O. Box 603, Fort Erie, Ontario L2A 5X3

Want to try 2 free books from another series? Call 1-800-873-8635 or visit www.ReaderService.com.

---

*Terms and prices subject to change without notice. Prices do not include sales taxes, which will be charged (if applicable) based on your state or country of residence. Canadian residents will be charged applicable taxes. Offer not valid in Quebec. This offer is limited to one order per household. Books received may not be as shown. Not valid for current subscribers to the Harlequin Intrigue or Harlequin Romantic Suspense series. All orders subject to approval. Credit or debit balances in a customer's account(s) may be offset by any other outstanding balance owed by or to the customer. Please allow 4 to 6 weeks for delivery. Offer available while quantities last.

Your Privacy—Your information is being collected by Harlequin Enterprises ULC, operating as Harlequin Reader Service. For a complete summary of the information we collect, how we use this information and to whom it is disclosed, please visit our privacy notice located at corporate.harlequin.com/privacy-notice. From time to time we may also exchange your personal information with reputable third parties. If you wish to opt out of this sharing of your personal information, please visit readerservice.com/consumerschoice or call 1-800-873-8635. **Notice to California Residents**—Under California law, you have specific rights to control and access your data. For more information on these rights and how to exercise them, visit corporate.harlequin.com/california-privacy.

HIHRS22R2

HARLEQUIN
PLUS

Announcing a **BRAND-NEW** multimedia subscription service for romance fans like you!

Read, Watch and Play.

Experience the easiest way to get the romance content you crave.

Start your **FREE 7 DAY TRIAL** at <u>www.harlequinplus.com/freetrial</u>.